# ALI CROSS

## LIKE FATHER, LIKE SON

# JAMES PATTERSON

1 3 5 7 9 10 8 6 4 2

Young Arrow
20 Vauxhall Bridge Road
London SW1V 2SA

Young Arrow is part of the Penguin Random House group of companies
whose addresses can be found at global.penguinrandomhouse.com

Penguin
Random House
UK

First published in the UK by Young Arrow in 2021
Published in paperback by Young Arrow in 2022

www.penguin.co.uk

A CIP catalogue record for this book is available from the British Library

ISBN: 978–1–529–12015–8

Printed and bound in Great Britain by Clays Ltd, Elcograf S.p.A.

The authorised representative in the EEA is Penguin Random House Ireland,
Morrison Chambers, 32 Nassau Street, Dublin D02 YH68

Penguin Random House is committed to a sustainable future
for our business, our readers and our planet. This book is made
from Forest Stewardship Council® certified paper

MIX
Paper from
responsible sources
FSC® C018179

2

6-2

# ALI CROSS
## LIKE FATHER, LIKE SON

**James Patterson** is the internationally bestselling author of the highly praised Middle School books, and the Ali Cross, Jacky Ha-Ha, Treasure Hunters, Dog Diaries and Max Einstein series. He also writes some of the most popular series of thrillers for adults, including the Alex Cross novels. James Patterson's books have sold more than 400 million copies worldwide, making him one of the biggest-selling authors of all time. He lives in Florida with his family.

# ALI
# CROSS Series

## Ali Cross

## Ali Cross: Like Father, Like Son

A list of more titles by James Patterson appears
at the back of this book

# ALI
# CROSS

## LIKE FATHER, LIKE SON

# CHAPTER 1

ALI CROSS, WHERE are you???

When I saw that text from my great-grandmother, Nana Mama, I got a bad feeling in my gut. Something told me my perfect day was about to come to a very imperfect end.

"Yo, I think I might have a problem here," I said, and showed my phone to Cedric.

He gave a low, bad-news kind of whistle. "Uh-oh," he said. "Tropical storm Nana Mama, moving in quick."

3

"Right?" I said. "If she finds out where I am, I'm toast."

The thing was, I'd told Nana Mama that I was going to be working on a report for school at Cedric's house that day. But it wasn't true. I mean, I *was* with Cedric. We just weren't anywhere near his house.

We were at the Anacostia Park Music Festival, having an awesome time with our friends. Ruby, Mateo, and Gabe were there, along with Ruby's best friend, Zoe. And if I'm being honest, I'd say Zoe was about 90 percent of the reason I'd gone AWOL in the first place.

I mean, I'd had crushes on other girls before, but this was the first time I'd ever thought one of them might actually like me back. That's what you call a miracle. So you could say there was a lot on the line.

We'd already stuffed our faces with cheesesteaks and fried dough, checked out a bunch of different acts, gotten our picture taken in this giant ANACOSTIA ROCKS photo frame, and even sat in on a steel drum lesson.

4

But none of that was the main event.

"You can't go *now*," Zoe said. "We're just getting started."

"I'm working on it," I told her, as we pushed through the crowd toward the main stage. "What time's your mom go on?"

Zoe looked at her phone. "Supposedly like an hour ago. But you know how it is."

I just nodded, like I knew exactly how it was to be the kid of a famous musician. Washington famous, anyway. People kept saying Zoe's mom, Vanessa "Dee-Cee" Knight, was going to hit the big time any day now. They called her the Queen of Go-Go, which is a homegrown Washington DC kind of music—a little funk, a little R&B, and a little old school hip-hop. It's not my usual jam, but again, I wasn't there for the music. I was there for Zoe.

So I doubled down with Nana Mama, and tried to buy a little more time.

Still working on my report at Cedric's, I texted back. I'll be home for dinner!

And don't get it twisted, by the way. I love my great-grandma, big time. But I'm not allowed to cross the Anacostia River without an adult. Not even to go to the park. Which was crazy. I mean, even Ruby and Mateo were allowed to be there, and their family's way stricter than mine. It was time for Nana to start figuring out I wasn't a little kid anymore.

"Let me see if I can find out what's up with my mom's show," Zoe said. "Give me five minutes. She's got to be back there somewhere."

Zoe pointed to the parking lot behind the stage. It was full of trailers, semis, and RVs, which I think were the dressing rooms. But it was also a restricted area. They had a long line of bike racks set up like a temporary fence to keep people out.

Not that it was going to stop Zoe. Already, she had her hands on that fence like she was ready to sneak over, no problem.

"Why don't you just go that way?" Ruby asked, and pointed at the actual backstage entrance, where a couple of uniformed dudes were checking IDs. "Just tell them your mom's headlining. They'll let you in."

"Yeah, no," Zoe said. "I'm allergic to cops."

The "cops" were really just security guards, but I didn't bother to correct her. I also didn't mention that my dad was a detective with the Metropolitan Police Department. Hopefully that wouldn't mean Zoe was allergic to me, too.

"I got this," she said. Then she started rapping, right there on the spot.

"Dee-Cee hanging back don't know where but gonna find out.

"Once she hits the stage gonna rage and blow your mind out.

"Watch me slip the line right on time here I go, yo.

"Quick as that there and back coming at you like a yo-yo."

"That was awesome," Mateo said, which it totally was. Zoe had a reputation at school for writing some dope poetry, and she could obviously freestyle, too. I guess it was in her blood, considering what her mom did for a living. Kind of like the way I'm always thinking about police procedure and crime scene investigation. (What can I say? I'm a cop's kid.)

"Don't leave before I get back," Zoe said, and

pointed right at me in a way that made my stomach jump. A second later, she'd slipped that fence like it wasn't even there, cut up between two of those big semitrucks, and disappeared.

I just stood there, watching the spot where she'd been, thinking about that sweet and salty smile of hers. And those gold box braids mixed in with the black ones. And the pink kicks she always wore. Let's just say Zoe Knight wasn't the type of girl you could easily miss in a crowd.

"I think *someone* likes you," Ruby said, as soon as Zoe was gone. "And I think their name starts with a Z."

"You *think*?" Cedric said, and he and Mateo fell on me, knocking me around and giving me a hard time. Not that I minded. Those two are my boys.

"She's super nice," Gabe said. "And really pretty, too."

Gabe's a little different, but I like how chill he can be, even if he is a typical gamer slash space cadet slash computer genius.

"I just hope Zoe gets back soon," I told them, because I knew the Nana clock was ticking.

And then sure enough, we'd barely been waiting

8

two minutes before the next text from my great-grandma dinged into my phone.

If you're at Cedric's house, why doesn't his mother know where he is???

"Aw, *man,*" Cedric said, reading over my shoulder. "That's what you call bad timing."

Nana wasn't playing, either. A second after that, my phone started ringing, with her name on the caller ID. I could practically feel the heat coming off the screen, just looking at it.

Mateo put his arms out, zombie style, and stumbled a few steps. "Nana…calls…must…obey…"

He wasn't wrong. But I also knew that if I had to leave before Zoe got back, I could kiss my chances with her good-bye. Which was probably the only thing I'd be kissing anytime soon.

"You going to answer that?" Gabe asked.

"Yeah," I said. I was just putting it off for as long as possible.

But then…everything changed.

I was just about to pick up Nana's call when a loud bang came from somewhere in that backstage parking lot.

It wasn't the kind of soft pop you hear sometimes. More like a hammer coming down on a piece of metal, which meant it was close by. Maybe four hundred feet, if I was guessing.

And in any case, I knew exactly what I'd just heard.

It was the sound of a single gunshot.

# CHAPTER 2

WHEN MY HEAD snapped in the direction of that sound, I was staring almost exactly the direction Zoe had gone a few minutes ago. But there was nothing to see, really. With all those trucks in the way, it was impossible to know what was going on. All we could know for sure was that Zoe was still back there—somewhere.

I felt like I'd just been wired with a thousand-volt current. I couldn't move, and my friends' faces looked like they were just as scared as I was. Not for ourselves, but because I think we were all wondering the same thing.

"What about Zoe?" Ruby asked.

People on our side of the fence weren't doing much, but everyone from the backstage area was coming our way. A couple of truckers knocked down a big piece of the barrier and kept moving, past us toward the river.

"Let's just make sure she comes back," Gabe said.

"She might be with her mom," Mateo said.

"And she might not," Ruby said, already working her phone. "She's not picking up, either."

We all stood there like statues, trying to make a decision about what direction to move in. But then Cedric decided for us.

"Come on," he said. He stepped over the place where the barrier was down. "We have to make sure she's okay. Watch your step."

There hadn't been any more gunshots, anyway. Just the one. The only banging now was inside my chest. My heart was going so fast it hurt. Still, there was no way we'd be splitting up. If I were Zoe in that situation, I'd want to know that my friends had my back.

A second later, we were following Cedric between the same two semis where she'd gone. It was like a canyon made out of trucks, and I couldn't see anything except what was straight ahead and straight behind.

"Where are those trailers?" Cedric asked.

"Maybe over there?" Mateo said, pointing. "Just keep going."

"And everyone stick together," I said. "No matter what."

When we came out of that truck canyon, there was a wide lane for driving, and then another row of vehicles and trailers. The whole place was like a giant maze, with no sign of Zoe.

"Zoe!" Ruby yelled.

"Zoe Knight!" Gabe added.

"Where are you?" Mateo yelled. But there was no answer.

We cut up between two more semis and kept going. So far, we hadn't seen anyone at all. As far as I could tell, nobody was back here anymore.

"Maybe we should turn around," Ruby said.

Except then I got one more idea. "Hang on," I said. I dropped flat to the ground and put my cheek down sideways. If I couldn't see through all those trucks, I could at least try to see under them.

Looking left, there was nothing but more parking lot. So I pivoted one-eighty, while the cement chewed into my hands and knees. That didn't matter, though, because as soon as I'd turned around, I spotted Zoe.

I couldn't see her face, but I recognized those pink J's on her feet right away. She was kneeling on the cement, a couple of rows over. And she wasn't alone.

Someone was standing there, facing her. A man, I'd guess, but I couldn't tell. All I could see were some heavy black work boots and the bottom of a long tan coat. I didn't know if they were talking to each other, or if something terrible was about to happen.

"ZOE!" I yelled as loud as I could.

"What is it?" Mateo asked. Everyone dropped to get a look for themselves. At the same time, whoever was in those black boots turned real quick, and moved off in another direction, out of sight—leaving Zoe behind.

*What* was going on?

The fastest way to her now was in a straight line. I didn't even think about it. I just stayed low and half crawled, half rolled under that big truck, then kept going, underneath the one next to it. Everyone else was right behind me.

When we all came out from under that second truck, Zoe was there, next to one of those dressing room RVs. It might have been her mom's, I didn't know, but there was no sign of anyone else. Zoe was still on her knees, looking dazed like she barely even knew we were there.

And that's when I noticed the blood.

It was dripping down her arm, over her hand, and making big red dots on the concrete. There was also an ugly black hole in the sleeve of her jacket, just above the wrist.

"You're hurt!" Ruby said. "Omigod...Zoe, are you shot?"

I could feel my breath coming up short while I tried not to panic.

"You guys?" Zoe's voice sounded weird, like it was coming from farther away than it was. Then she looked down at her arm, just before she collapsed the rest of the way to the ground.

I couldn't believe it. I couldn't even imagine this was actually happening.

And the only people around to help Zoe right then were us.

# CHAPTER 3

"ZOE? ZOE?" I yelled. "Can you hear me?"

Zoe looked around at us with this weird expression, like she was sorry for something. Her right hand was gripping her left wrist. The blood was still soaking her sleeve, and she had a splatter of it on her cheek, too.

"Ali?" She reached out like she wanted to get up, but I put a hand at the back of her head and got her to lie down instead.

"Call 911!" I said.

"I already am!" Ruby said. She had a hand pressed over her ear so she could hear. "Hello? Hello? Are you there?"

"Where's your mom?" Gabe asked.

"I dunno," she said. "Couldn't find her..." She was mumbling, and working just to get the words out. I wondered if she was in shock. Was that even a thing for a wound like this?

Cedric and Mateo were flanking us on either side. Gabe looked like he was going to be sick, but he hung in next to me, cradling Zoe's head while I moved down to her arm.

My heart was thundering. I knew I had to keep Zoe calm. Even more important, though, I had to stop her bleeding.

"Put your hand up," I told her, and helped her slowly raise the wounded arm. "That's it. Just keep it above your heart."

It was like my brain had gone into autopilot. The words coming out of my mouth felt like they were coming from someone else. But the fact was, I knew what to do. I'd been absorbing this stuff all my life, watching two zillion episodes of *Law & Order*, reading like crazy about detectives and emergency responders, and surfing YouTubes on crime scenes and first aid for as long as I could remember.

Still, there's YouTube and then there's real life. I just prayed I wouldn't mess this up, because it didn't get any realer than this.

"Hello?" I heard Ruby again behind me. "My friend's been shot! We need an ambulance right away. We're at the Anacostia Park Music Festival, in the parking lot behind the main stage! Please, please hurry!"

Meanwhile, I needed something for a bandage to put some pressure on the wound. I couldn't just use my hands.

"Cedric, hold her arm for a second," I said.

He grabbed on and I yanked my DC NATIVE sweatshirt over my head as fast as I could.

"Okay, let me back in there," I said.

I wrapped one of the sleeves three times around Zoe's wrist. Then I put my hands around the whole thing and squeezed as tightly as I could.

Zoe groaned.

"You're hurting her!" Mateo said.

"I'm sorry!" I said. "It's how you're supposed to do it."

"Just…do what…you need to…" Zoe gutted out, taking a breath every couple of words. I couldn't believe how strong she was. If it were me, I think I would have passed out by then. Even now, I felt like I was going to blow my lunch.

"We got you, Zoe," Gabe said. He had his hands on her feet, and he sounded calm enough, but I could tell he was just as scared as me. Everyone was either crying or trying not to.

"Where's that ambulance?" Ruby asked. She was looking around, but the two trucks on either side of us were making it just as impossible to see as ever. So Cedric and Mateo took off in both directions, to try and get a wider lookout. Ruby stayed on the phone with 911, while Gabe and I stuck with Zoe. It had only been a minute but it already felt like forever.

"Zoe," I said, leaning close now. "Who was that I saw?"

"Huh?" she asked.

"Someone was standing right here with you a second ago," I said.

"Don't know...what you mean," she said.

I looked at Gabe, but he was looking over his shoulder, trying to figure out what was going on.

"Someone in a long coat," I started to say, but she cut me off.

"No!" she said, and tried to sit up again. It was intense, the way she was looking in my eyes now. Not like before.

"Lie back," I told her, and made her put her head down again. Then I leaned in close and put my ear where I could hear her.

She only whispered this time. Her voice was rough, and I could tell she was scared.

"Whatever you thought you saw, you're wrong. Okay?"

I glanced at Gabe, but he just looked confused. I had no idea what was going on, if she was lying for some reason, or if I'd made some kind of mistake about what I thought I saw.

Except, no. It wasn't that. I *knew* what I saw.

The only other thing I could tell for sure was that Zoe was in a bad way. Not just because she'd been shot. Something else was part of the picture here, and she was desperate not to talk about it.

*Why?*

I had a million things running through my head, but Zoe didn't need me agitating her right now.

*"Okay?"* she said again, like she really needed an answer.

"Yeah, okay," I told her. I didn't feel like I had a choice.

"Good," she said, and seemed to ease up just a little bit.

"Just hang in there," I said. "Help's coming. It won't be long now."

"Nah," she said, and gave me a tiny smile with her eyes closed. "Help's here. Thanks for looking out for me."

"You got it," I said, and smiled back even though I felt tears burning in the corners of my eyes. I could hear sirens now, coming closer. Lots of sirens, in fact.

Hopefully, at least one of them was for us.

# CHAPTER 4

"OUT OF THE way, kid!" someone said.

I didn't even realize a police officer had gotten there until I was making room for him to take over the compression on Zoe's arm.

"The ambulance is here, too!" Cedric yelled out.

"We got you, Zoe!" Ruby said. "You're gonna be okay!"

"Hi, Zoe, I'm Officer Weyland," the uniformed cop told her. "Can you hear my voice?"

"Mm-hm," Zoe said. Her eyes were still closed, and she sounded almost sleepy or something.

"Okay, good job, sweetheart. I just need you to hang in there another few seconds for me—"

"I ain't your sweetheart," Zoe grunted out, and the cop laughed like she was joking, even though I don't think she was.

"That's the spirit," he said. "Good job. Just stay with me."

"What about your mom?" Ruby asked her. "Where do you think she is?"

"Don't know," Zoe said. "Couldn't find her. Wasn't picking up."

"Everyone's being evacuated," the cop said. "Don't worry, we'll track her down. You'll see her at the hospital."

Everything felt like it was rushing by and moving in slow motion at the same time. I watched the EMTs move in, and felt Gabe's hand pulling on my arm as Officer Weyland started telling us to step back.

"Can I go with her?" Ruby asked, but the cop shook his head.

"Family only," he told us. All we could do was

24

watch as they loaded her into the back of the ambulance.

"We love you, Zoe!" Ruby shouted after her, but I don't know if she heard. A second later, they'd closed the doors and Zoe was on her way to the hospital. I didn't even know which one.

It was all too much to think about at once. None of this felt real—the gunshot, the chaos in the park, all of it. But mostly, I couldn't even start to figure out why Zoe had reacted the way she did when I mentioned the person I'd seen. The one who may or may not have been the shooter, but definitely walked away from her *after* she'd been shot.

It made no sense. Then again, a lot of crimes seem that way at first. Sometimes, the things that don't add up are just pieces of a bigger puzzle and you need to find the other pieces before you can start to see the whole picture.

That's what I was counting on, anyway.

We were standing in a tight group now. Ruby and Mateo were holding hands, and Cedric had his arms around Gabe's and my shoulders. We needed to be strong for Zoe and for each other, too.

"You kids see anything?" Officer Weyland asked us. He had a little pad and a pen out, like the kind my dad carries to crime scenes. I knew it was Weyland's job as first responder to start asking questions right away, and that MPD detectives would take over once they got there.

In the meantime, I had to decide how much to say. We all did. And from the way Gabe kept looking at me, I still couldn't tell if he'd heard what Zoe had told me. Either way, nobody spoke up.

"Listen, guys," the cop said. "I need your help, and I need to know what happened to your friend."

"We didn't see anything," Gabe said then.

I didn't correct him, either. There had to be a reason Zoe was so desperate for me to keep my mouth shut. But what was it? The only thing I knew for sure was that if I spilled the truth now, I couldn't take it back. And Zoe was the victim here. Not anyone else. She deserved the benefit of the doubt. For all I knew, she was still in some kind of danger.

"Come on guys, *think*," the cop said. "Let's start with what you were doing when that gunshot went off. Where were each of you?"

"Excuse me, sir," I said. "But are we required to answer your questions?"

"Pardon?" the cop said.

"Are we being detained?" I asked. I knew our rights, and I knew that the cop did, too. He could ask everything he wanted, but unless he was taking us into custody, there was nothing in the law that said we had to talk, or even stick around.

After a long pause and a deep breath, he finally answered me.

"No," he said. "You're not being detained."

Meanwhile, Ruby, Gabe, Mateo, and Cedric were all looking at me like this was some game of follow-the-leader and I was at the front of the line. None of them were saying a word.

"So are we free to go?" I asked. My heart was picking up speed again. I could hear my voice, confident on the outside even though I felt like a bowl of cherry Jell-O on the inside.

The officer looked me in the eye one more time. And when he looked away, I knew we were in the clear. For now.

"Go on then," he said.

I wasn't trying to make trouble. It felt more like I was trying to do the same thing he was—protect the victim. And if I was making a huge mistake right now, at least I was going to make it in the name of doing what was right for Zoe.

Either way, I wasn't going to forget what I saw, not that it was that much. Just someone wearing a pair of black work boots and a long tan coat. Still, as soon as I had a chance, I intended to get all over this thing.

And I wasn't going to stop until I had some answers.

# CHAPTER 5

THE AMBULANCE HAD barely left when my phone rang. I saw my dad's name on the screen and picked up right away.

"Dad?"

"Are you okay?" he asked. "Your great-grandmother said you disappeared in the middle of a conversation and that you're not answering her texts."

"I'm okay," I said. "Well, I mean ... actually ..."

"Where are you?" he asked.

"Anacostia Park," I said.

"*What?* I just heard on my radio there was a shooting there."

"There was. It's a friend of ours, Dad. Zoe Knight. She got shot in the arm."

I heard Dad take a breath. "Is anyone else hurt?"

"No, sir. I'm with Ruby, Mateo, Gabe, and Cedric. They just took Zoe to the hospital. We weren't allowed to go with her. It's pretty crazy here..."

I had to stop talking because I was getting this big lump in my throat, like everything that had just happened was pouring down on me at once. I felt one of my friends squeeze my shoulder. It almost hurt, which meant it had to be Cedric.

"Just sit tight," Dad told me. "All of you. I'm already on my way. Where in the park are you?"

"Anacostia Drive and Good Hope Road," I said.

"Be right there."

The park was emptying out quick. Cops with flashers and neon vests were directing cars out of the area and sending foot traffic toward the Eleventh Street Bridge. I knew an Evidence Response

Team would be here soon, but so far, I didn't see any ERT jackets on the cops who had shown up. This was a big, wide-open space. They were going to need a big team to preserve it, cover it, and investigate it. And while one part of me wished I could stay to observe and ask questions, another part of me couldn't wait to get out of there. It was hard not to feel a little scared, even now.

"You guys okay?" I asked everyone after I hung up.

"That was insane," Cedric said. "Poor Zoe."

"I've never seen a real gunshot wound before," Mateo said.

"Me, neither," Ruby and Cedric both said.

It was true for me, too, but I noticed Gabe didn't say anything at all. Something told me this wasn't his first time.

A minute later, I heard Dad shouting from close by. "Ali!" I looked over and saw him coming to a stop on the side of Anacostia Drive. He had a red flasher rolling on the roof, which is how he'd gotten past the roadblocks at either end of the park. "All of you kids! Get in!" he shouted.

I jumped in front. Ruby, Cedric, and Mateo squeezed into the back. And Gabe, who's even smaller than me, got in the way back.

"Thank God the rest of you are okay," Dad said. "Who's this friend of yours, Zoe?"

"Zoe Knight," Ruby said.

"Her mom is Dee-Cee Knight," I said.

"*The* Dee-Cee Knight?" Dad asked. I knew he was a fan. He and my stepmom, Bree, had even gone to see her a few times at Twins Jazz, one of the last great spots for music on U Street. That's the part of the city that used to be called Black Broadway. And Zoe's mom's shows always sold out there.

"She was supposed to play the festival this afternoon," Ruby said. "That's what we were all doing there. I'm even writing a report about her for school. Zoe was going to introduce us and everything."

"I thought that's what you were doing today," Dad said to me. "Working on your report, at Cedric's."

I didn't know what to say to that. I'd lied about it to Nana Mama, and now Dad knew about it, too. I didn't even have a topic for this paper yet, even though it was going to be a third of my social studies grade. But that seemed like the least of my worries right now.

"Do you know where they took Zoe?" I asked instead.

"Howard," Dad answered. That meant Howard University Hospital, up in Northwest DC. But we weren't going that far. All of us lived in the Capitol Hill section of Southeast, and Dad was taking everyone straight home, including me. At least he didn't keep the heat on about my lie.

"Detective Cross, do you know if she's going to be okay?" Gabe asked.

"I'm sorry, kids. I don't know anything yet," Dad told us. "You said she was hit in the arm?"

"In her wrist, I think," Mateo said.

"That's right," I said.

"Hopefully there won't be any broken bones," Dad said. "But it sounds like it could have been worse."

"Could have been a lot worse," Cedric said. "Like...well..."

He never finished that sentence. I don't think anyone wanted to think about it.

As for me, I was wrestling all over again with what to say. Or more like what *not* to say. It was one thing to keep my mouth shut with some cop I didn't know. It was a whole other thing with my dad, like sitting on the world's most uncomfortable secret.

But still, I'd made a promise to Zoe. So I made a deal with myself, right there. I'd sit on this for twenty-four hours, period. No more. If I could get to Zoe before then, maybe I could get a clue about what the heck this was all about. And if not, then I'd come clean.

It didn't make me feel any better, but it was something, anyway.

"Ali?" Dad said.

"Huh?" When I looked up, I realized I'd stopped listening to everyone and gotten lost in my thoughts. It happens all the time, to be honest.

Dad was pointing at the back of my hand. "There's some napkins in the glove compartment. You want to wipe that off?"

I looked down and saw a bunch of little dots, running up from my hand to my elbow. There was more on my shirt, too. I don't know how I'd missed it before, but as soon as I realized I was looking at Zoe's blood, my whole insides heaved.

"I'm going to be sick!" I said.

Dad started to pull over but I was already rolling down the window. A second later, I was blowing a whole afternoon's worth of junk food all over the Eleventh Street Bridge. Like that day hadn't been bad enough already.

But at least it meant there weren't any more questions on the way home.

# CHAPTER 6

DAD DROPPED EVERYONE else off first, then took me to our house on Fifth Street. When we pulled up in front, Nana Mama was there on the stoop. For all I knew, she'd been standing like that for an hour, waiting to see me.

"I'm going to run over to the hospital," Dad said. "You go take a shower. Maybe lie down for a little while. Whatever you have to do. We'll talk more later."

"Yes, sir," I said. I felt kind of weak and shaky, like I'd run all the way home instead of getting a ride.

"Hey," Dad said, and I looked over. "You okay?"

"Yeah," I said. "I mean, not about what happened to Zoe. But me? Yeah, I'm okay."

Still, Dad put the car in park and cut the engine.

"What are you doing? I thought you were going to the hospital," I said.

"That can wait," he said. "You're my priority right now. And Zoe wasn't the only one to take a hit today. This happened to all of you."

It was getting more uncomfortable by the second. The more time I spent with Dad right now, the more time I was going to spend *not* telling him what I probably should have been saying all along—that I might have actually seen the shooter.

"Seriously, Dad," I went on. "I know I should be freaked out, but the thing I'm thinking about the most is Zoe. So if you're asking me what I need right now? That's what it is. I need to know how she's doing. Please?"

Dad looked at me for another long stretch. And just when I felt like I was about to cave and start blabbing, he nodded.

"All right," he said, starting up the car again. "You're the boss, but only for now. We'll talk later, got it?"

"Yes, sir."

"Whenever you're ready."

"Thank you, Dad."

"And hey, Ali?"

"Yeah?"

He grabbed me hard, and pulled me close. "I love you, son. You're my blood, and don't ever forget that."

"I won't," I said. "I love you, too." The words got kind of mushed up against Dad's chest, but I think he got the idea.

After that, I went up the stoop and straight into another long hug, this time from Nana. She's got some old lady core strength, I'll tell you that much, and she squeezed me like she wasn't ever letting go.

"Oh my, oh my, oh my," she said. "You must have been so scared."

"I'm sorry I lied about where I was, Nana," I said. "It's just that..."

"Shhh. That's nothing we have to talk about today," she said. My sister, Jannie, was there now, too, hugging both of us. Mr. Arnold across the street was staring hard out his window, but I didn't care.

"Ali? Are you okay?" Jannie asked.

"I'm okay," I said. It seemed like the easiest answer, even if it wasn't completely true.

Then Nana stood back and gave me a look, up and down. "How about you go get washed up?" she said. "Then come down for dinner later. Or I'll bring you a plate, if you like."

The last thing on my mind was food, but Nana was right about the first part. I needed to wash off before anything else happened. And then I needed to find some time to myself, so I could start sorting through all the questions jangling around inside my head.

Because that's all I had right now—way too many questions. And not nearly enough answers.

# CHAPTER 7

WHEN I GOT out of the shower, there was a group
text waiting for me.

RUBY: Can you guys get together right now? Usual spot?

GABE: Already there.

CEDRIC: Give me two seconds.

I texted back to everyone while I headed downstairs to the basement.

ALI: Be right there.

I knew Nana Mama was around somewhere, and
it wasn't going to fly to just walk past her without

some kind of excuse. So I put my phone to my ear and started talking.

"Hello?" I said, as I passed the empty living room and went up the hall toward the kitchen. I could see Nana now, sitting at the table.

"Hey, man," I said to nobody on the other end. "How's it going?"

Nana looked up from her crossword puzzle and smiled at me as I passed through. I smiled back and held up a finger to say *just a second*.

"Yeah," I said into the phone. "I might have it downstairs. Let me check."

Then while Nana went back to her puzzle, I opened the basement door, started down, and closed the door behind me. I pocketed my phone now that I was in the clear.

Thirty seconds later, I had my headset on and I was logging in to my PS4. I opened a new game of *Outpost*, clicked through the welcome screen, and fast-traveled to our usual meeting spot, which was Gabe's base station. We each had a home base of our own inside the game, but Gabe was like some kind of *Outpost* genius. His place was by far the sweetest

41

crib I'd ever seen anyone build. He even had some tunes going when I got there. I could hear Drake playing over my headset, along with my friends' voices.

It was kind of crazy, I know. We didn't have to get inside a game just to talk to one another, but it was like a habit. And Gabe's place was like our headquarters.

My avatar was called Cassius Play, and I could see QUB (Gabe), Lowkey-Loki (Cedric), Blackhawk (Ruby), and Cagey-B (Mateo) literally just sitting around in their own skins, too. It looked like walking into the teachers' lounge at the Justice League.

But I wasn't here to play or make jokes.

"Hey, guys, I'm here," I said.

"Any word from your dad on Zoe?" Ruby asked.

"He's still at the hospital," I said. "I'll text you all as soon as I hear anything."

"I don't get it," Mateo said. "Who would do this? Nobody hates Zoe."

"Maybe it was just random," Gabe said. "Maybe it was some psycho trucker or something."

"Right?" Cedric said. "She goes back there looking

for her mom, maybe sees some guy by his rig, doing something he wasn't supposed to be doing—"

"Like what?" Ruby asked.

"I don't know," Cedric said. "I'm just saying, I agree with Mateo. It's not like Zoe's got some secret life of crime going on."

"I don't think it was just a random shooting," I said. Or more like I blurted it out. I'd been holding so much in, it was like I'd just sprung a leak.

"Why don't you think so?" Ruby asked.

"Because I might have seen something, or... someone," I said.

"What?" Ruby practically shouted.

"I don't know yet," I told them. "It wasn't much, but when I asked Zoe about it, she begged me not to say anything."

"I *thought* something was going on," Gabe said.

"Why'd she ask you not to say anything?" Cedric asked.

"I don't know," I said. "I don't know anything right now. I have to talk to Zoe first and try to find out."

"What'd you see?" Ruby asked.

I felt guilty for talking about this at all, but it seemed even more wrong to keep quiet at this point. At least these guys were there when it happened. So I laid out all the details I could remember—the black work boots, the long coat, and how whoever it was had been standing over her until we shouted Zoe's name.

"And then they just walked away," I said. "I don't even know if it was a woman or a man."

"A man," Ruby said. "A woman wouldn't do this to her."

"Don't be so sure," Mateo said.

I wasn't going to get into it. The point was, I'd kept some important secrets from Ruby, Mateo, and Cedric in the past, and I'd really regretted it. I wasn't going to make that mistake again.

"Seriously, though, you guys," I said. "None of that info leaves the group. Not until I get to talk to Zoe, okay?"

"What is this?" Cedric asked. "Another case for the Ali Cross detective agency?"

"Why not?" I asked. "It's better than sitting around waiting to find out what happened."

"I'm down," Ruby said.

"Me, too," Cedric said.

"Me, three," Gabe said. "Look what you guys got done last time. If it weren't for you, I probably wouldn't be sitting here right now."

I wasn't going to point that out myself, but the truth was, Gabe's disappearance earlier that year had turned out to be my first "real" investigation. I mean, not *real*, since I'm just a kid. But at the same time, it's also true that I was the one to find him in the end. Maybe sometimes it takes a kid to investigate a kid's problem.

Like maybe right now.

"You guys want to re-up?" Cedric asked then. "Maybe start an actual game here, until we get some more info from Ali's dad?"

"Not for me," Ruby said.

"Yeah, I think I'm going to go chill," Mateo said.

"Text as soon as you hear anything," Gabe reminded me, just before we all started logging off and disappearing from the screen.

Not that I was done thinking about all this. Instead, I went back to my room, flipped open my

MacBook, and created a new file that I called ZOE. Then I started writing down the truckload of questions I had running through my head.

> WHO DID THIS TO ZOE?
> WHY?
> WHO DID I SEE WITH HER? WAS THAT PERSON THE SHOOTER?
> ANY CAMERAS IN ANACOSTIA PARK?
> OTHER WITNESSES?
> SUSPECTS? FAMILY MEMBERS? ENEMIES?
> WHY DID ZOE ASK ME NOT TO SAY ANYTHING?

That last question was the big one right now. It was probably going to keep me awake all night. But at the same time, I realized, the question itself was a clue.

If Zoe wanted me to keep her secret—whatever it was, exactly—that meant she knew something she wasn't telling. And chances were, *that* meant she

46

knew who fired the gun. Maybe even knew them personally.

I couldn't prove anything yet, but it was a start. Now I just needed to figure out a way to get to her in that hospital. I didn't know how yet. I just knew that's what I had to do.

Somehow.

# ALEX CROSS

ALEX CROSS SHOWED his police credentials to the sleepy attendant at the third floor desk of Howard University Hospital. The woman stifled a yawn as she handed him a pink card for admittance to the pediatric ward.

"Long day?" Alex asked.

"Honey, you don't know the half of it," she said.

"Oh, I might," he answered with a dark smile, as he waited for her to buzz him through.

A second later, the large sweeping doors at the

pediatrics entrance peeled open, clearing his way to the corridor beyond. Straight ahead was the nurses' station, with rows of hospital rooms along both sides of the hall. Family members in street clothes and a few kids in hospital gowns were moving about, but mostly it was quiet. An empty gurney sat near the entrance, with a silver GET WELL balloon still tied to its side rail.

Zoe Knight's room wasn't hard to spot. A uniformed police officer was stationed outside the door, which meant one thing. Whoever had put poor Zoe in the hospital was still out on the street somewhere. In any case, she'd be perfectly safe here. Alex just hoped Zoe would get whatever help she needed, both medically and emotionally. He knew all too well that bullets could leave behind more than one kind of scar.

"Has it been quiet?" Alex asked, flashing his badge for the officer.

"So far, but it's lighting up on the news right now," the cop told him. A tilt of his head indicated the television mounted near the ceiling of Zoe's room in the far corner. On the screen, a Channel

Four reporter was standing in front of the hospital delivering a live broadcast.

"Anacostia Park and the surrounding area have been closed off until further notice. Word from the unnamed victim's medical team is that they expect her to make a full recovery. Meanwhile, according to our sources, community leaders tonight are gathering to craft a response to this shooting. We'll have more on this emerging story as it develops. Reporting live from Howard University Hospital, this is Rhea Sloan for Channel Four News at Six."

Alex nodded to the cop and leaned inside the hospital room. He could just see Zoe now, sitting up in bed. Two adults were there, seated on either side of her, and they stood up quickly as Alex appeared. The man was unfamiliar to him, but the woman was immediately recognizable. This was Vanessa "Dee-Cee" Knight, one of Alex's favorite local performers.

"Can I help you?" she asked with a protective edge in her voice. She wore a dark-brown leather jacket and matching pants, with her hair braided back over one heavily bangled ear.

"Ms. Knight? Zoe? I'm so sorry to bother you," he said. "I'm Ali Cross's dad..."

"Mister, I don't care who you are—" Dee-Cee started to say before Zoe spoke up.

"Momma, wait!"

The girl sat halfway up before the man eased her back against the pillow. "Easy there, girl," he told her. Zoe's right arm was bandaged in white gauze and suspended in a blue sling. Her braids were in the same style as her mother's, but shorter, barely reaching the collar of her yellow-and-white hospital gown.

She ignored the man and turned straight to face Ms. Knight.

"Momma! This is that boy's daddy. The one who..." She stopped short, as if she'd just realized something. Then she looked Alex right in the eye. "Ali's the one who saved me today," she said.

Alex felt a warm swell of pride in his chest, but he kept a straight face.

"Oh, my god," the mother responded, and came right over. She put her hands on both of his elbows and held on tight. "Excuse my rudeness. It's been a day."

"Not at all," Alex said. "I'm sorry to barge in."

But the woman was still talking. "*Thank you,* sir. Thank you for that boy. Let's just say you did something right when you brought him into the world."

"I can't disagree with you there," Alex said. "But Zoe, how are you doing? Ali tells me you were a champ today."

"That's my Zoe," Dee-Cee said. "My stainless steel warrior child."

Alex could just hear the distinctive, gravelly alto of the woman's voice, and even the hint of a songwriter's poetic word choice when she spoke. He couldn't help smiling at that.

"I hope you don't mind my saying, I'm a fan," Alex told her.

"Well, thank you for that, too," Dee-Cee answered with a modest smile of her own. Then she turned to the other man in the room with a gesture. "This is my manager, Darnell Freeman."

"Good to meet you," the man said, with a smile and a handshake.

"You, too," Alex said, and turned his attention back to the girl in the middle of them all. "How are you feeling, Zoe?" he asked. "Ali and your other friends are counting on me to bring them some good intel. Any messages for the team?"

"I'm all right," she said. "My wrist is broken, but I guess it could have been a lot worse. Oh, and tell Ali I owe him a sweatshirt."

The girl was remarkably centered, all things considered. Alex had a good feeling about her, which was nice, considering his other hunch—that Ali had a crush on little Zoe. Not that his son would ever admit it. Ali tended to play his cards close to the vest.

"And you don't know who did this to you?" Alex asked.

"No, sir," Zoe answered right away.

"None of her friends saw anything, either," Dee-Cee added.

"That right?" Zoe asked, with a glance at her mother. Something about the exchange caught Alex's attention. Zoe had seemed almost glad to hear it.

"Well," Alex said. "I don't want to take up too much of your time. Let me give you a card, and if there's anything I can do to help, or anything you remember, Zoe, I want you to feel free to call me."

Zoe craned her neck to see the card as he handed it to Dee-Cee.

"Hold up," she said. "Are you police?"

Mr. Freeman took the card from Dee-Cee and looked at it next.

"Sorry, yes," Alex said. "I didn't mean to be unclear about that. I really am here as Ali's dad, but like I said, if there's anything I can do—"

"Thanks," Zoe said, maybe a little too quickly this time. She obviously had some feelings about the police, whatever those might be.

"Yes," Dee-Cee echoed. "Thank you for everything, and please tell the same to your son. I can't wait to meet him."

"Of course," Alex said. A new question had just pushed into his mind, but he didn't want to overstay his welcome. And besides, something in his gut was telling him to wait. *Not now. Not yet.*

So he kept the thought to himself, at least for the

time being. Still, it stuck with him all the way down in the elevator and back to his car in the parking garage. He couldn't prove anything right now, but he also couldn't dismiss the question itself, which had to have shown up for one reason or another.

*Why was Zoe Knight lying about this shooting?*

# CHAPTER 8

**WHEN I CAME** down for breakfast the next morning, the TV was on in the kitchen. Which was weird right away. We're never allowed to watch TV during family meals.

But today was different. I could hear a reporter from the news before I even came in the room.

"Residents in Southeast Washington are responding this morning to the shooting of a middle school–age girl at the Anacostia Park Music Festival yesterday afternoon. It marks the sixth shooting of a minor in the District this year alone, including one fatality. Today, community members are asking for answers."

I stayed just outside the kitchen, listening. Something told me my family would turn this off if they knew I was there, and I wanted to hear more.

Next came a man's voice. An angry one.

"Gun violence in Washington is out of control," he was saying. "That's just a fact. We are sick and tired of seeing our children pay the price while the city's government and police department do *nothing* to stop it."

Nana clicked off the TV. "Enough of that for now," she said.

"Leave it on," I said, coming into the room. "I wanted to hear that."

Everyone looked over at the same time, like I was sick and supposed to be in bed or something.

"Good morning," Bree said.

"Come have some breakfast," Dad told me, without turning the TV back on. Nana had the waffle iron going, and I could smell apple and chicken sausage in the pan. I wasn't going to say no to any of that.

"I can't blame people for being angry," Nana went on, putting a bowl of cut fruit in front of me for a starter. "But I know you all are doing your best over at MPD."

"Honestly, if a little pressure from the community is going to make us do better, then I'm all for it," Dad said.

"But the police aren't the bad guys," Jannie said. "It's the people who are making these shootings happen."

"It's complicated, for sure," Bree said.

"Still, thanks for the vote of confidence," Dad told Jannie, and kissed the top of her head. Then he turned and looked at me. "We've gotten a few calls for you this morning, as well."

"For me?" I said. "From who?"

"From the press," Dad said. "Word's getting around that you stepped up for Zoe in a big way."

Jannie slid her phone over to show me something.

On the screen it said, DC COP'S SON PLAYS HERO IN
LOCAL SHOOTING.

This was just getting weirder and weirder. I didn't
feel like a hero, including when I'd been bandaging
Zoe's arm with my sweatshirt. Mostly, I'd just felt
scared.

"Where'd you find this?" I asked Jannie.

"Some blog," she said. "But those calls were legit.
One of them was CNN. You should do an interview,
Ali. People want to talk to you."

I looked at Dad to see what he was thinking.

"Up to you," he said. "Either way, we're incred-
ibly proud of how you handled that situation. If
you're interested, I'll let you do *one* interview, but if
not, that's completely fine, too."

I didn't want anyone interviewing me. I didn't
even want anyone thinking about me right now.
What I wanted was to be left alone so I could figure
out a way to get to Zoe and talk to her in private.

"Do they know anything more about who did
this?" I asked Dad.

"Not as far as I know," he answered. "But I'm

not on this case. I think Lars Matheson is heading it up."

Still, I wasn't sure how much Dad could tell me, even if he did know. So I just cut to the chase.

"Hey, Dad, can I go over to Gabe's this morning?" I asked.

"Why? What's up?" he asked.

"Nothing," I said. "I just want to get away from all this mess for a little bit. You know. Chill. Play some *Outpost*. Whatever."

"You need to be working on your report," Nana said. "The one you did *not* work on yesterday, even though you said you were. We still have to talk about that."

I noticed Dad, Bree, and Nana looking at one another now, like maybe they didn't all agree about whether to bring that part up.

I just kept still and looked Dad right in the eye like nothing sketchy was going on. But on the inside, I felt like dog doo for keeping so much of the truth a secret.

*Just this one more time,* I thought. *Then I'll come clean.*

At least, that's what I told myself.

"Yeah, sure," Dad said. "But check in. Two hours, okay? Put it in your phone."

I set the reminder without any argument. I still felt guilty, for sure, but there was no going back now. Only forward.

Next stop, Howard University Hospital.

# CHAPTER 9

AFTER BREAKFAST, I stuck in my AirPods and headed out the back door. At the gate to the alley behind our house, I turned left like I was going to Gabe's, in case anyone was watching from the kitchen.

But then I went the long way around on Sixth Street and doubled back toward the Navy Yard Metro stop. That's where I was really going.

From there, it was a straight shot on the green line up to the hospital. I rode with Migos, Lil Nas X, Major Lazer, and a bunch of others pumping in my ears. And pumping me up for what I had to do next, too.

All of that was the easy part. I had no trouble finding my way to the hospital's third floor, and getting myself as far as the entrance to the pediatrics ward. The hard part was going to be getting inside.

The big double doors that led to the ward had to be buzzed open by a lady at the reception desk, I saw. And according to the sign, you had to be eighteen to get in there alone.

I barely look my own age, much less eighteen. And besides, I didn't want to draw too much attention to myself. So I took a seat in the waiting area while I tried to figure out my next move.

I sat in one of the plastic chairs they had, with a view of the elevators and the ward entrance. I couldn't see the receptionist, but that meant she couldn't see me, either, which was good. If anyone asked, I was just going to say I was waiting on my parents. Meanwhile, I kept my head down, with my eyes and ears open.

It didn't take long to learn the drill. Visitors got

off the elevator, went to the desk, and signed in for a pink admittance card. Then the lady would press some button she had, and the pale blue doors would swoosh open automatically.

I watched that happen a few times, and then on the third go-round, I counted it off in my head. The lady pushed the button. The doors opened. And—

*One...*

*Two...*

*Three...*

*Four...*

*Five...*

*Six...*

*Seven...*

*Eight...*

On nine, the door swooshed shut again. This was going to be tight, but not impossible.

Now I just had to be patient, like a real detective on a stakeout. My dad's been stuck on surveillance details for as long as twelve hours at a time. It takes focus, patience, and, sometimes, a really strong bladder. At least I had a bathroom I could use if I needed.

But in fact, it was only twenty minutes later when I got my shot.

That's when I saw a Black couple about Dad and Bree's age getting off the elevator. If I played it right, they'd never even know I was there, and everyone else would just see some kid with his folks.

As they went and got their passes, I stood up and walked over toward the elevator like I was leaving. Then I paused, like I was looking at something on my phone, even though I was really listening in.

"Good morning, can I help you?"

"Hi, we're Tracy Bennett's parents, here to see our daughter."

"Of course. Please just sign in here."

My nerves bumped way up now. But I was excited, too. I kept thinking about how Zoe had slipped over that fence the day before. If she were doing this, she probably would have been past those doors a long time ago.

A few seconds later, I heard a familiar buzzing sound. *Swoosh,* the doors opened and I started the count in my head.

*One . . .*

*Two...*

The couple crossed the hall toward the entrance, talking as they came.

"Maybe we should have brought something."

"It's okay. She just wants to see us."

*Three...*

*Four...*

"What she wants is to come home."

"I know, babe. I know."

They were just passing through the open doors now.

*Five...*

*Six...*

I pivoted the long way around, enough to give me a quick look at the reception desk, where the lady was already talking to someone else.

*Seven...*

*Eight...*

The coast was as clear as it was going to get. I kept moving and slipped through the doors behind my "parents," right before—

*Nine...*

*Swoosh,* the doors closed up behind me. Just

like that, I was in. And the couple I'd followed had already peeled off down the hall to the left, leaving me on my own. Sweet!

*All right,* I thought. *Don't get cocky. Stay sharp.* Because I wasn't done yet. In fact, looking straight ahead, I could see that I still had to get past one more very big obstacle.

The kind with a uniform and a badge.

# CHAPTER 10

DAD HAD MENTIONED there was a cop stationed by Zoe's room, so I wasn't surprised by it or anything. I just wasn't sure how to get around him.

The thing I needed to avoid was staying in one place for too long, looking suspicious. Instead, I kept it moving, and kept my street face on, too— eyes front as I walked slowly down the hall like I hadn't even noticed that cop.

Unlike the rest of the hospital, the walls in here

were bright colors—orange on one side and green on the other, with planets and stars painted along the ceiling. That was nice, I guess, but it still smelled like floor cleaner and Band-Aids to me. Hospitals kind of creep me out.

I didn't look at the cop as I passed him. I just walked right on by and then, super casually, looked back over my shoulder into the room.

Zoe was sitting up in her hospital bed with a bright-pink cast on her arm. She had a notebook on her lap, with a pen in her good hand. And for a fraction of a second, our eyes met.

"Ali!" she shouted.

I stopped then and looked straight at the cop as he stood up from his chair. Unlike Zoe, he didn't seem so happy to see me.

"It's okay! He's my cousin," Zoe called out without even missing a beat. "Ali, come on in!"

I checked the cop again, and he just shrugged. "Go ahead," he said, so I scooted on past him before he could change his mind.

"Close the door," Zoe told me, which I did, and

then went over to the side of the bed. It was weird to see her in a hospital gown, like catching her in pajamas.

"I thought you were allergic to cops," I said, thumbing over my shoulder and trying to make a joke.

"Yeah, like I got a choice," Zoe said. "He just leaves me alone, and that's fine by me."

"Where's your mom?" I asked.

"Down in the cafeteria with Darnell and my auntie," Zoe told me.

"Darnell?"

"He manages my mom's career. Bookings, getting paid, stuff like that," she said.

"Oh. Cool," I said. I wondered what it was like to have a mom with a manager, and a YouTube channel, and actual fans.

"What about you?" she asked. "Where's your dad?"

"At home, I guess," I said, and Zoe's eyebrows went up. I think that's when she knew I'd snuck out to see her. Maybe it earned me a little respect.

"Does your arm hurt?" I asked.

"Not really," she said, even though I'll bet it did. Zoe was tough that way. It was good to see her sitting up and smiling, too, after that crazy scene at the park. But I knew I had to hurry. There was no knowing how long we'd have that room to ourselves.

"Hey, so Zoe? Can I ask you something?" I said.

"Yeah?" she said, like she wasn't so sure.

"It's about what happened yesterday," I said. "Who was that I saw you with?"

"I still don't know what you're talking about," she said.

"Someone in black boots and a long coat," I told her, pushing past how uncomfortable I was getting. "Is that who did this to you?"

Zoe's face didn't change. She just shook her head a little. "Whatever you thought you saw, you didn't. Okay?"

I noticed it was almost exactly the same words she'd used the day before. That only made me more curious.

"Maybe I saw someone you missed," I said. "I mean, you weren't exactly in good shape just then. Maybe you..."

I didn't even finish my sentence. Zoe wasn't listening anymore, or even looking at me. I thought she'd get heated then, or tell me to leave, or both.

Instead, she held up the red spiral notebook that had been sitting on her lap. I recognized it right away. She was always carrying that thing around school, scribbling in it during lunch, or in the hall, or pretty much anywhere she went.

"I wrote something for you," she said, flipping through the pages.

"What is it?" I asked. I had no idea where this was going, but I definitely noticed she'd changed the subject.

"It's kind of a poem," Zoe said. "I mean, it doesn't rhyme, but still."

"Can I hear it?" I asked.

"Nah." She tore out one of the pages and handed it to me. "But you can have it, if you want."

Her handwriting was crazy neat. Not like mine. And the title at the top of the page was just "Ali." Which made my face heat up all over again, even before I started reading the rest.

ALI

They say Muhammad Ali was
the greatest of all time.
Boxer, activist, humanitarian.
And I suppose it's true.
But this boy who shares his
name
will always be The Greatest to
me.
Hero, warrior, savior.
A gentle-handed, fierce-
hearted fighter,
he rained blows down on my
fear,
threw jabs at my suffering,
took down my need,
and knocked it straight out.
Anyone else might have walked
away from that fight,
but not him.
Not this boy.
Not Ali.

I am
forever
grateful.
—ZK

Now I felt even weirder than before, kind of
happy and embarrassed at the same time. It was like
my head was too crowded to sort everything out at
once.

"Wow," I mumbled. "That's super dope. I appreciate it."

"I appreciate you, Ali," Zoe said. And the thermo-
stat behind my face kicked up another few degrees.

"How'd you even know I'm named after Muhammad Ali?" I asked.

"Ruby told me," she said. Which I guess meant
they were talking about me at some point. But now
I was just standing there like an idiot with nothing
to say. I wasn't good with words like she was. Especially around girls. And extra-especially around Zoe.

"I just want you to know," she kept going, "whatever else happens, I'll never forget what you did for
me. Ever."

*"Whatever else happens?"* I asked. What was that supposed to mean? "What's going to happen?"

But that's as far as I got.

"Who's this?" someone said behind me. I turned around and recognized Zoe's mom coming into the room with a couple of other adults.

"Momma, this is Ali," Zoe said.

And just like that, the one and only Dee-Cee Knight wrapped me up in this big, long hug while everyone watched. Like I wasn't already uncomfortable enough.

"Bless you, boy," she said. "You ever need anything from this family, all you've got to do is ask."

"Yes, ma'am," I said. "Thank you, Ms. Knight."

"No," she said, stepping back. She was just as pretty as her daughter. "I'm *Dee-Cee* to you. Got it? I ain't kidding, Ali Cross. I owe you one, and trust me when I say, we Knights don't ever forget what we owe."

"Truer words," said the man with her. I guessed that was Darnell, the manager. He was big, with two diamond studs in his ears, and reminded me of Delroy Lindo, one of my dad's favorite actors. "Well done, Ali," he said, shaking my hand. "Very well done."

I guessed that the other lady was Zoe's aunt, but she hung back and didn't say much.

Meanwhile, my little hospital visit was coming to a quick end. I was going to have to take off without getting anything I'd come for. Except getting to see Zoe, of course, which was really nice. I just hoped that what I had to do next wasn't going to mean the end of whatever friendship we'd been starting up.

Because it was time for me to go home and come clean with Dad.

# CHAPTER 11

"DAD? ARE YOU up here?"

I was mad nervous when I got home, climbing the stairs to his office in the attic. But the longer I waited to tell what I had to tell, the worse it was going to get.

"Come on in," he said, and I sat myself on the old yellow and brown couch with all the stuffing coming out of it. He's had that thing in his office since before I was born.

"There's something you should know," I said. "About Zoe."

Dad saved his work on the computer and then turned to give me his full attention. "What is it, bud?"

I took a deep breath and went with it.

"I saw someone at the park yesterday," I said. "Standing with her after that shot went off."

*"What?"* Dad exclaimed. He'd heard me, but I think he was just surprised. He kept his cool, anyway, and ran a hand over his chin like he does when he's thinking. "Why have you been sitting on this?"

Even now, I was juggling different parts of the story in my head. I still didn't want to tell him I'd been to the hospital if I could help it.

"Zoe begged me not to say anything," I confessed. "I know someone was there with her, but she kept saying it wasn't true. I think she's in trouble, Dad."

Dad thought about it some more. In the silence, I could hear Nana running the vacuum all the way downstairs, while I waited to see how mad he was going to get.

But then he surprised the stuffing out of me. Just like that couch.

"I had a feeling about this," he said. "I think she's in trouble, too."

I was seriously stunned. Even though I didn't know what to expect, it definitely wasn't that.

Dad went on. "Did you see this person fire a gun? Or holding a weapon?" he asked.

"No, I didn't even see their face," I said. Then I gave him all the details I had, which wasn't much. "By the time we got to Zoe, whoever it was had disappeared. I can't even say for sure if it was the shooter, or someone else, or what."

Dad was nodding the whole time and taking it in.

"Why do *you* think she's in trouble?" I asked him. "Did something happen when you were at the hospital yesterday?"

He didn't answer, though. I knew he couldn't tell me. He was the cop, and I was just the kid. But still, my brain was spinning like a hamster wheel. And yeah, I was a little bit psyched that Dad and I had come to the same conclusion, too. It made me feel like I was on the right track.

"I'll get on the phone with Detective Matheson as soon as I can," Dad said. "He's going to want to talk to you."

"But..." I wasn't sure how to respond. "I promised Zoe I wouldn't say anything. I'm only telling you because—"

Dad cut me off right there. "This is bigger than one promise to your friend, Ali. We can't sit on it, legally or otherwise. And listen..."

He rolled his chair over to where I was sitting and leaned in with his hands clasped.

"I wish you'd told me this yesterday," he said. "I know you've been through a lot, but don't you ever withhold information like that again. Understood?"

My chest felt hollow inside, half guilty and half scared. I'd kind of thought I was going to get away without this part of the talk.

"I'm sorry," I said. "I really didn't know what to do. But what about—"

"We'll talk more later," Dad said. "Right now, I need to call Detective Matheson, so why don't you head on downstairs?"

I guess, if anything, I was glad Dad didn't get

more upset than he did. I just hoped I'd made the right decision to tell him, and that it wasn't going to bite me in the butt. Or even worse, make more trouble for Zoe.

"Hey, and Ali?" he said, stopping me at the top of the stairs. "You can tell me anything, anytime. I mean that. *Anything.* Okay?"

I thought again about how I'd snuck off to the hospital after I told him I was going to Gabe's. It made my chest feel just a little hollower than before. This whole thing was getting more complicated all the time, in more ways than one.

"Yes, sir," I said. "I hear you."

But that's all I said.

# ALEX CROSS

ALEX WAITED UNTIL Ali had gone downstairs before he picked up the phone to call Detective Matheson.

"Lars, it's Alex Cross," he said. "I just got word from my boy, he's been sitting on something he didn't disclose until now."

"What is it?" Matheson asked.

"I had a feeling about this when I left the hospital last night. Sounds like Zoe Knight knows more about this shooting than she's telling. You don't have to share your take on it with me. I know this is your case, but I can bring Ali in for a chat, if you'd like."

Alex passed on the details as he'd gotten them from Ali.

"Sounds like she might be protecting someone, or even herself," Alex said. "I know that can happen for a lot of reasons, but is there anyone you know of who might be holding something over her?"

"We're looking at a long list," Matheson replied. "There's an ex-boyfriend of the mother's. Also, Zoe's father. A few other family members. A business manager. I don't want to go too deep into it right now."

"Who's this ex-boyfriend?" Alex asked, just on a gut feeling.

"The name's Orlando Fletcher," he said. "Dee-Cee called the cops on him a few times when he was living there, but the responding officers only put it down as domestic strife. No arrests, anyway."

"Still, he sounds like a real prize," Alex said.

"That's not all," Matheson answered. "He also has a nine-millimeter weapon registered in his name."

That was the same caliber weapon that had been used against Zoe, Alex knew.

"Ballistics isn't showing a match to the slug we recovered," Matheson said. "But it means this guy likes a nine mil. And where there's one, there might be another."

"What about Dee-Cee's manager?" Alex asked. "Darnell Williams?"

"Nothing's flagging there. At least not yet, anyway. He's been working with Dee-Cee for three years now. But in any case, we're not ruling anything—or anyone—out."

"And the father?" Alex asked, but that was met with a long pause. In the silence, Alex could sense he'd asked one too many questions.

"Listen, Cross, I appreciate the input, but I've got to keep moving. You understand, right?" Matheson said, not really asking so much as telling him that their conversation was over.

Alex didn't like it, but he understood. Matheson was a young detective, more new school than old. The collaborative, groupthink investigations Alex was used to were falling by the wayside. Everyone was a lone wolf these days, it seemed. But bottom line, it was Matheson's case, and Matheson's call to make.

That much, Alex could respect.

# CHAPTER 12

WHEN DAD HUNG up with Detective Matheson, I
waited for him to turn his music back on. Then I
turned slowly away from the bottom of the attic
stairs and tiptoed to my room.

I probably shouldn't have listened in on that call,
but what can I say? I was in deep, and I couldn't
pass up the chance to learn as much as possible.

Not that I'd gotten that much. Basically, what I
had now was a small persons-of-interest list, based
on what I'd already been thinking about, combined

with what I'd just heard. So I opened the ZOE file on my laptop and put it in writing.

*Dee-Cee Knight*
*Darnell Williams*
*Zoe's father*
*Dee-Cee's ex-boyfriend*

I didn't think for a minute that Zoe's mom was behind this, but as an investigator, you can't assume anything, and you can't rule stuff out just because you want it to be that way. Parents and spouses are *always* people of interest.

I didn't know anything about Darnell Williams, either. Just that he was Dee-Cee's manager, which meant he was probably at the park for her show when that gunshot went off. It didn't automatically make him a suspect, but it sure didn't rule him out, either.

That left the other two on my list. I didn't even have names for them, but I did know who to ask about it. So I picked up my phone and fired off a text to Ruby.

ALI: Hey, you know anything about Zoe's dad, or about her mom's ex bf?

87

RUBY: Not really. I think her dad's out of the picture. She never talks about him.

ALI: What about the ex?

RUBY: Orlando something. Zoe HATED him, for whatever that's worth. I don't know the last name, but I can ask her if you want.

ALI: Not yet. I don't know if Zoe should even know we're doing this.

RUBY: Doing what?

I sat there and tried to think of a way of putting it so it wouldn't sound like I was going after Zoe. Because I wasn't. The fact was, we needed to know as much about her as we did about everyone else. So I just texted back a straight answer.

ALI: Investigating her. For her own sake.

A second later, my phone rang. It was Ruby calling.

"What in the *world* do you mean?" she said. "*Investigating* Zoe?"

"Well, yeah," I said. "I'm not saying she did anything wrong. But something's definitely going on, and if she can't say what it is, then the best way for us to help her is to find out on our own."

"Wow," Ruby said. "That's kind of heavy, Ali."

"So's getting shot," I said.

"Word." I heard her take a long, deep breath. "Can I tell Mateo about this?"

"For sure," I said. "Mateo, Cedric, Gabe. But that's it. We need to keep this locked down as much as possible."

"Hundred percent."

The more I talked to Ruby about it all, the more it sounded like that persons-of-interest list was going to get a whole lot longer before we were done. According to Ruby, Dee-Cee and Zoe let people use their house a lot. There was always someone writing at their kitchen table, or big family dinners happening, or background singers rehearsing at the piano, and I didn't even know what else.

"Do you know anyone who has something against her?" I asked.

"Against Zoe?" Ruby said. "No way. Seriously, that girl wouldn't hurt a fly."

"Maybe not," I said, "but I'll bet she knows someone who would."

After we hung up, I started googling everything I

could think of, but didn't get very far. There weren't any stories I could find about Dee-Cee Knight and this Orlando dude, whoever he was. I'd have to keep digging on that.

And I didn't do any better with her father, either. It was just dead ends for now. So I texted Gabe next and asked him to look into it. If any of us could do a deep dive, it would be him.

When I ran out of names, I even started watching a bunch of Dee-Cee Knight videos. She was really good. I could see why Dad and Bree liked her stuff so much.

One of her songs was called "Hoops." At the beginning, it showed these girls taking off their earrings, and you think they're about to get in a fight. But then they're really just getting ready to play some ball in the park. It was kind of great, actually.

Even better, when it came to the credits at the end, I saw where it said LYRICS BY ZOE K. KNIGHT. And yeah, I was impressed. A lot.

I also wondered what the K. stood for, just because I'm curious that way. It was like for every scary thought I kept having about Zoe's situation, I had another thought about how much I liked this girl.

Bottom line, I knew Zoe didn't *need* me to save her. She was about as strong as they came, and besides, who was I to even think I *could* save her if I wanted to?

But man, I sure did want to.

# CHAPTER 13

I COULD FEEL it when I walked into school the next morning. Something was different.

Sure enough, as soon as I got past security, I saw a big poster in the front hall with a picture of Zoe on it. The word ENOUGH was printed across the bottom in red letters, along with WASH LATIN LOVES ZK inside a heart.

Word had obviously gotten around. I even had some people come up to me in the hall and tell me they'd heard about what I did.

"You're a hero, bro. Way to go," Keith Sanders said as I passed by. There was that word again. I heard it a couple more times before I got to morning advisory, too.

My homeroom teacher, Mrs. Achebe, always started the morning with us sitting in a circle at the back of her room. She had a bunch of beanbag chairs and pillows there, so we could "ease into the day," as she sometimes said.

"So, does everyone know about what happened to Zoe Knight over the weekend?" Mrs. Achebe asked. And every single person did.

Patrice Shimm spoke up first. "It isn't right. Black people are getting shot all the time in this city, and the police don't do anything about it."

A bunch of people nodded at that, but I just kept still.

"I heard you were there," William Carter said, looking at me. "Is that true?"

"Yeah," I answered. I didn't mind if anyone wanted to ask questions, but I wasn't going to be offering up any stories on my own.

"Do you want to say anything about it, Ali?" Mrs. Achebe asked. "It's completely up to you."

"I heard you saved her life," Destiny Sweeney said.

"It wasn't like that," I said. "I mean, she was hurt, for sure, but I just... did first aid."

I wasn't trying to be fake-humble about it, either. I just couldn't match up what they were saying with what actually happened. And besides, it seemed like we should be talking about Zoe, not me.

"Do you know how she's doing?" Mrs. Achebe asked.

"She's got a broken wrist," I said. "And she's still in the hospital, but I think she's okay. Or at least, she will be."

Nobody said anything then. I noticed Destiny wipe her face on her sleeve, and Mrs. Achebe handed her a tissue.

"It's messed up, though," Jamal said next. "I mean, *Zoe Knight*?"

"Right?" Jasmine Washburn said. "Things ought to be different around here. It's frustrating."

"Is there anything you kids think you could do about that?" Mrs. Achebe said.

"Yes," Patrice said.

"And no," Jasmine said, and the two of them fist-bumped. We all knew this was more complicated than just one simple answer.

Patrice tried again. "I mean, kids are protesting and doing stuff all over the country."

"Right, but it's the rich White kids who get all the attention," Jasmine said. "Black kids have been protesting gun violence for a lot longer than just what you see on the news."

"That's exactly right," Mrs. Achebe said. "So let me ask again. Is there anything you all think you can do?"

The bell rang before anyone could really get into it, but Mrs. A made us promise to put that one in the parking lot. We'd be talking more about it later.

Then, as we were filing out for first period, Mrs. Achebe called me over to her desk.

"How are you doing, hon?" she asked. "I was a little surprised to see you show up for school today."

"I'm okay," I said. I felt like that's all I'd been saying since Saturday afternoon. I wanted to shout it loud enough for the whole world to hear—I'M OKAY, I'M OKAY, I'M OKAY—just so people would stop asking.

But of course, I didn't do that. I knew Mrs. Achebe was just looking out for me.

"Have you thought of writing about this for your social studies assignment?" she asked. "Gun violence *is* a part of life in Washington."

That was the assignment, to write something about "My Washington." But I still hadn't figured out what "My Washington" meant for me yet.

"I don't know," I told Mrs. A. I really just meant *no*, but I didn't want to get into it.

"All right," she said. She didn't make me explain, which I also appreciated. "I'm here, if you want to talk, or brainstorm, or, you know. Whatever else."

And of course, I knew what she meant by "whatever else."

"Thanks," I said.

"Love ya, Ali. Take care of yourself, okay? That's not just a bumper sticker. I mean it."

Mrs. Achebe never held back, and never treated us like we were little kids. I kind of loved her back, but I never said so. That was just too goofy.

"I gotta go," I said. Then I scooted out the door and up the hall to math, just like it was any other day. Even if it wasn't.

# CHAPTER 14

IT HAPPENED FASTER than anyone thought. Word
started circulating that morning, and then at twelve
noon exactly, four hundred and thirty-two kids
walked out of Washington Latin Middle School.

I didn't have anything to do with making it happen, but yeah, I walked out along with everyone
else. People were ready to make a statement and
they weren't waiting around for the adults to help
them make it.

We started on the steps in front of the school, but pretty soon those filled up and we had to move across the street to the playing fields.

The whole thing wasn't supposed to be more than half an hour, and whoever had pulled it together chose Mekhi Thomas to speak for the student body. He was president of the eighth grade, and pretty good at firing people up, too.

And I guess someone had made some calls, because by the time it got started, three news vans had shown up, along with maybe half a dozen other people with cameras and mini-recorders.

Once everyone was on the field, Mekhi got up on the bleachers with a bullhorn that I'm pretty sure he got from the main office.

In fact, when I looked around, I noticed our principal, Mr. Garmon, and Mrs. Achebe, and a whole ton of other teachers and school staff watching from around the edges. Technically, this walkout was against the rules, but they weren't doing anything to stop it.

I was standing near first base with Cedric and

Mateo. Ruby was over with her girlfriends, and I was guessing Gabe was still inside. This wasn't his kind of thing. He's not the walkout-and-shout type.

"We may be kids in the eyes of the law," Mekhi said over the bullhorn. "Or in the eyes of our teachers, or parents, but we're also citizens of this city. Am I right?" Everyone cheered and clapped at that.

"We're not *trying* to be adults," Mekhi went on. "We're not *trying* to be kids. We're just living our lives. Ain't nobody here setting out to get shot just going to school, or out to the park on a Saturday afternoon, if you know what I mean."

He was talking about Zoe, of course. That's why I was there. For her sake.

"But guess what? It can happen. And we live with it, because we don't have a choice."

"That's right!" people were yelling.

And "Go on, Mekhi!"

And "That's what it is!"

It was totally lit, but also peaceful. This felt like exactly what everyone needed right now.

Including me. I was shook after what happened to Zoe, but I was mad, too. I hated that she had to go through this, and it helped to be out there on the field with everyone else. They were mad, too.

Mekhi went on. "That's what you hear all the time," he said, while those cameras rolled and the rest of us listened. "They say, 'there's nothing we can do,' and 'that's just the way it is.' And they keep selling it like that, and we just keep on buying it, like that's the deal we're supposed to make. But guess what? Starting today, I say *no deal*. I say there *is* something we can do. In fact, we're doing it right now!"

"No deal!" some people started yelling, and Mekhi picked it up with the bullhorn, until everyone was chanting it together. You could probably hear it all over the neighborhood.

"No deal! No deal! No deal!"

"We need *basic* gun safety laws put into place," Mekhi said, getting back at it, while people kept cheering.

"We need to feel safe, coming to and going from school," he said, and the cheering got even louder.

"We need a police department that cares about kids like us," he added. And this time, it turned into a lot of booing. Not for Mekhi, but for the police.

That part felt like a punch I should have seen coming. I could feel some people around me looking my way just then, too. They knew who I was.

"Don't trip," Cedric said, right up at my ear. He was seeing the same thing I was. "Just ignore them."

But then Patrice decided to push it a little further, even while Mekhi was still going.

"What do you think about that, Ali?" she called over, with a little handful of her friends right there, backing her up.

"Don't start," Mateo told her, but I answered anyway.

"I think it's true," I said. "MPD can definitely do better. But that doesn't mean every cop is bad, or that the department doesn't care about what happened to Zoe."

I had the attention of a few more people now. So did Patrice, and she knew it.

"What a shock," she said. "Ali Cross, defending the police."

"I'm just saying, it's complicated," I told her.

"And by the way, shut up, Patrice," Cedric said.

"Good one, Cedric," she said back, sarcastically.

"Come on." Mateo started pulling both of us away. "It's not worth getting into."

"Yeah, walk away," Eddie Cruz said, because Mateo was pulling on my arm. My blood was pumping, too, and I'm glad he was there to step in. I didn't want to say anything I'd regret. And I knew better than to get into a fight on school property. That hadn't done me any favors the last time it happened.

But I also knew that wasn't the end of it. In fact, something told me this was just another beginning. And not in a good way.

# CHAPTER 15

THAT NIGHT, WE all had spaghetti with Bree's famous meat sauce for dinner, followed by brownies that Jannie had made for dessert, along with vanilla ice cream and hot fudge. It was really nice, like the first normal thing to happen since Zoe got hurt.

But then, during dessert, Nana took out a map of the city and unfolded it on the table. I saw she'd marked it up with red and green magic marker, all around Southeast and Capitol Hill.

"What's this?" I asked.

"Moving forward, I want to be as clear as possible about what is and is not acceptable," Nana said. "I thought some kind of visual aid might help."

Nana used to teach school for like forty years, so this was exactly her kind of thing. She liked charts and graphs and maps. And she liked things to be crystal clear, too.

Dad and Bree were there, of course, but this was Nana's call. She's the one who kept track of me during the day. Or anytime the two of them weren't around, which was totally unpredictable with Dad's job. It's not like Washington's bad guys only work from nine to five.

"This is serious, Ali," Nana told me. "We're not going to punish you for sneaking out to that music festival, although maybe we should. But we *are* going to have a talk about where it is and isn't okay for you to be on your own."

"I wasn't on my own," I said, even though I knew what she'd say.

"And you weren't with an adult, either," she told me.

True enough. But I guess I just wasn't in the mood.

"This is so dumb," I said. "I *know* I'm not supposed to cross the river. We've talked about it a million times."

"Well, apparently it's going to take a million and one for you to get it," Nana said. "This isn't an inquisition, Ali—"

"I didn't say it was—"

"Excuse me? Do not interrupt like that," Nana said.

"Sorry."

Dad squeezed my shoulder. He wasn't going to take my side, but I could tell he knew this wasn't easy for me. Still, they weren't going to let me be disrespectful, either.

So I tried again. "Seriously, Nana. I really am sorry. I just wanted to go to this thing with my friends, and I knew you wouldn't let me. But to be honest, I think you worry too much. Like for real."

Bree and Dad looked at each other now, and then over at Nana.

"I see," she said, taking her time. "Well, I'll be honest with you, too, Ali. That might have meant something more to me before what happened to

Zoe on Saturday. And I know you don't want to hear this, but after your deceptive behavior on top of that, I'm inclined to worry just a little bit more."

It was so frustrating, almost the same way it had been with Patrice and her friends. It wasn't like I thought Nana was crazy, just like I didn't think Patrice was making it up that the police department had some real problems. I could see all that.

In other words, I could see Nana's point. I just wasn't sure she could see mine.

Maybe it was just the day I'd had, but my eyes were starting to sting. The last thing I wanted right now was to start crying when I was trying to tell her I wanted to be taken more seriously.

"You're awfully quiet," she said. "Is there anything else you want to say?"

"Yeah," I told her. "See, my rules haven't changed since fourth grade. That's messed up. I mean, I know I'm still a kid, but I'm not a *little* kid anymore. And you just keep on acting like I am."

"Yes." Nana sighed and folded her hands. She even looked a little sad herself now. "You've told me that a thousand times."

Something inside me kind of melted just then. Not because we'd figured anything out, but because I hated to see Nana Mama feeling bad. No matter what happens, I can never stay mad at her for more than a second.

But I couldn't resist getting in the last word, either. I scooted over and leaned right up against her then, and took a bite of her dessert. Just like I used to do when I actually *was* a little kid.

"Well, I guess it's going to take a thousand and one," I said.

# CHAPTER 16

WE MET ONLINE at Gabe's home base every night now. It was like our regular thing. We barely even played *Outpost* anymore.

That Wednesday, Gabe was the first to report in. He'd done some deep diving, and according to him, this ex-boyfriend of Dee-Cee's was named Orlando Fletcher.

"How'd you figure that out?" Mateo asked.

"You've just got to know where to dig," Gabe said. He could do more with Google than anyone I knew. "I'm pretty sure he's working at a place called Nubuilt Garage in Southwest. Unless it's a different Orlando Fletcher."

"No, that sounds right," Ruby said. "I think he's some kind of mechanic."

"When did he and Dee-Cee break up?" I asked.

"She kicked him out about two months ago. Zoe practically threw a party when she did," Ruby said. "Hey, and speaking of parties, Dee-Cee's having one at their house on Saturday. Z got out of the hospital last night, and this is like a welcome home thing. But also a thank-you for everyone who's been helping out. She wants you all to come."

"Seriously?" Gabe asked. You could tell he wasn't used to getting invited to things.

"I wonder if any famous people will be there," Mateo said. "Dee-Cee know anyone with the Wizards?"

"Yeah, cause that's the whole point," Ruby said. "So you can get yourself an autograph."

"I'm just saying—"

"Yeah, yeah."

I was glad to hear Zoe had gotten out of the

hospital, but I also wanted to stay focused on what we'd been talking about.

"So anyway," I said, "we already have means and motive on Orlando. Now we just have to think about opportunity."

"Say what?" Cedric asked. "Is that some kind of detective thing?"

"Actually, yeah." It was something I'd picked up from Dad, listening to him talk about all his different cases over the years.

"We know Orlando Fletcher owns at least one gun," I explained. "In other words, he had the *means* to do this. And since Dee-Cee kicked him out, I'm guessing he wasn't too happy about that. Which could give him a *motive*."

"Why would he go after Zoe, then?" Gabe asked. "Why not Dee-Cee?"

"Maybe to get back at her?" I said. "I don't know, but the real question now is whether he had the opportunity to fire that shot."

"In other words, does he have an alibi, or could he have been at Anacostia Park on Saturday at four-fifteen?" Ruby said.

"Exactly," I said. "Cedric, you want to go over to Nubuilt Garage with me this weekend and see what we can find out?"

"You know it," Cedric said.

If our team had a head of security, Cedric would definitely be it. He was always up for anything. He was also a foot taller than me and looked like a high schooler. Exactly the kind of kid you want at your six when it counts.

"Next question," I said. I had my laptop with me, and I was making notes the whole time. "What about Zoe's dad? You get anywhere on that, Gabe?"

"Not really," he answered. "Dee-Cee's Wikipedia page says she was married to someone named Stephen Knight for eight years. But I can't find anything on him. It's like he doesn't exist. Not online, anyway."

"Weird," Cedric said.

"Zoe's never said anything about him?" I asked.

"Not to me," Ruby answered.

"Gabe, can you keep looking?"

"Yeah." I could already hear him keyboarding in the background.

"Who else are we looking at?" Mateo asked.

"Well, we know Dee-Cee and Darnell were at the park at the right time," I said.

"And I think Kim was there, too," Ruby added.

"Who?" I asked.

"Zoe's aunt," Ruby said. "She's Dee-Cee's sister. You met her at the hospital."

"So that's who that was," I said. I remembered the lady who came in with Dee-Cee and Darnell, but she'd mostly hung back that day.

"Kim lives with them and takes care of Zoe when Dee-Cee's on the road," Ruby said. "But Ali, she'd never do something like this in a million years. Same for Dee-Cee."

"I hear you," I said. "This is about people of interest, not suspects. There's a difference. And since I'm about ninety-five percent sure Zoe knows the person who did this to her, we shouldn't rule anyone out until we have actual proof. That's just good investigative procedure."

"Dude, you are such a geek," Mateo said.

"Geeks are gonna rule the world," Gabe said.

"Yeah, well you'd know," Cedric said, and we all busted out laughing.

So maybe we were just a bunch of kids, but I felt like we were actually getting somewhere, working together like this. Dad would call it *old school*. He's always saying how detectives these days act like free agents and spend more time working on their computers than they do with one another.

Not me, though. Because if old school was good enough for Alex Cross, then it was definitely good enough for me.

Hopefully for Zoe, too.

# ALEX CROSS

ALEX CROSS WAS parked at his desk on the third floor of MPD headquarters when word came around. Detective Matheson was bringing in a suspect on the Zoe Knight shooting.

According to the desk sergeant, it was Orlando Fletcher, the ex-boyfriend of Dee-Cee Knight. Everyone knew Alex had a stake in this one, and also that Matheson tended to keep his cards close to the vest.

"Thanks for the heads-up," Alex told Sergeant Rook. "Where are they taking him?"

"They're just getting started up in the fourth floor interview room," Rook said. "But you can watch from down here."

The interview room cameras were all patched into the building's Wi-Fi, and accessible from computers on the third, fourth, and basement levels. Alex didn't waste any time. He slipped right down the hall to the nearest observation suite on the north side of the building.

Three desktop screens provided the only light in the tiny room. Alex took a seat in the gloom and logged on to the system. After entering his password, a grid of small black-and-white video feeds appeared, and he clicked into the one for Room 4C.

It showed him a wiry, fit-looking man—presumably Orlando Fletcher—sitting at a metal table across from Detective Matheson. Fletcher's posture was a picture of indifference. One arm crossed his chest with the other hand on his chin, while his left leg jutted straight out from the chair where he sat.

"I'm going to start with the most obvious question," Matheson was saying. "Where were you on Saturday afternoon?"

"I've got nothing to hide, man," Fletcher responded.

"So then answer the question," Matheson said.

"It's like I already told you," Fletcher said. "I was home watching tennis all afternoon."

Matheson barked out a short laugh. "I don't know, Orlando. You don't seem like the tennis type."

"Yeah, well, you don't seem like..."

"What?" Matheson said.

"Never mind."

Fletcher had obviously been about to say something he was going to regret. So he wasn't a complete loose cannon. But he *was* here for a reason.

"So you're telling me you were home all afternoon on Saturday, and that nobody saw you, or even talked to you the entire time?" Matheson asked.

"It's what I said, isn't it?" Orlando shot back.

"When was the last time you saw Dee-Cee Knight?" the detective asked next.

Fletcher ran a hand over his chin and left it there. When he spoke, it was through his fingers.

"I don't know, man. February something. It was the day I moved out of that house."

"The day she kicked you out," Matheson corrected him. "Sounds like you two had a pretty rocky relationship, including a couple of police calls to the house."

"Whatever. I ain't seen her since."

"What about her daughter, Zoe?" Matheson said.

"Nah," Fletcher said, shaking his head. "Why? She done something, too?"

Matheson ignored the question. He stared at Fletcher for a long time and let the silence ride. Or maybe he was just figuring out his next move.

Eventually, the detective stood up to leave the room. "I'll be right back," he said. "Don't go anywhere."

"Like I got a choice," Fletcher said, just before the heavy metal door slammed closed, locking him inside.

While Alex waited for whatever came next, he logged in to a second computer and pulled up Zoe's case file. There was nothing inappropriate about reading departmental records, and it certainly wasn't against the rules.

*Matheson probably wouldn't like it,* Alex thought. But that was Matheson's problem.

According to the case notes, multiple witnesses had seen Dee-Cee Knight in the wings of the music festival's main stage at the same moment that the city's ShotSpotter program had recorded a single gunshot that day—the same one that had broken Zoe's wrist.

Which meant Dee-Cee was in the clear. It wasn't surprising, but it was good news all the same.

Darnell Williams and Kim Lafountain—Dee-Cee's manager and sister—were more up in the air. Both of them had been at Anacostia Park, but their whereabouts at the time of the shooting were unconfirmed.

Meanwhile, it didn't look like Detective Matheson had enough on Orlando Fletcher to hold him much longer. Certainly not enough to book him into custody. Alex was going to be very surprised if Fletcher didn't walk within the hour.

Still, it was progress. And if Alex had to guess, he would have said that Detective Matheson was correct in his suspicions.

Orlando Fletcher had "primary suspect" written all over him.

# CHAPTER 17

THE NEXT DAY, Zoe was back at school. She was like a mini-celebrity, and everyone was happy to see her, but Ruby and her girls kept tight around her all morning.

I didn't even get to talk to Zoe until just before fourth period. And even that was by accident. I was coming down the back stairs for gym and heard her voice before I even saw her.

"Okay, that works," she said. "I'll see you at four. Love you, Daddy. All right. Bye."

That word—*Daddy*—jumped right out at me.

We'd just been talking about this. Even Ruby didn't know anything about Zoe's father.

I leaned over the railing and saw her in the back corner. We're not allowed to use our phones in school, so I guess she was hiding out.

"Hey!" she said, and came to meet me at the bottom of the stairs. "I'm sorry I haven't talked to you yet. It's been a minute."

"No worries," I told her. I mean, yeah, I wanted to talk to Zoe all the time now, and not just because of the investigation. But it wasn't like I expected to be her top priority. "How's your arm?"

"Itchy," she said, and waved that pink cast at me. "I've got to deal with this thing for six weeks. I can barely even text."

I pointed at her phone. "Were you just talking to your dad?" I asked. I couldn't help throwing out the question. I was too curious.

"Nah," Zoe said, like it was nothing. "Why?"

"No reason," I said. "Must have heard wrong."

But that was the thing. I *hadn't* heard wrong. And I was pretty sure she knew that I knew it, too.

The question was, why did Zoe need to lie about

her dad? And more important, did it have anything to do with the other secrets she'd been keeping?

Or, was I just sticking my nose in where it didn't belong? That was completely possible, but there was only one way to find out. Already, I had a new idea bubbling up in my brain.

Meanwhile, a bunch of people were coming down the stairs now. When Zoe saw them, she picked up her backpack and took a step toward the main hall.

"I'm late for math," she said, even though the bell hadn't rung yet. It seemed obvious to me that she wanted to get out of there. Maybe because I'd asked one too many questions. "You're coming over on Saturday, though, right?" she asked.

"Definitely," I said.

"Good. I'll see you then," she told me.

"See you Saturday," I said.

But I had a secret of my own now, too. The truth was, I'd be seeing Zoe a lot sooner than Saturday night. More like three-thirty that afternoon when school let out.

And if everything went the way I wanted it to, she wouldn't even know I was there.

# CHAPTER 18

THAT DAY IN social studies Mrs. Achebe checked in with everyone about the big reports we were supposed to be writing.

"You should all have your topics approved by this Monday, so you can start writing next week," she said. "And let me remind you, this project counts for one-third of your final grade."

I still hadn't decided on a topic. It was hard to come up with anything I felt passionate about, which was supposedly the idea.

"Mrs. Achebe?" Patrice said. "Can I do something a little different?"

"Depends on what you mean," Mrs. Achebe said.

"You're always asking us what we can do to make things better in the world, and I have an idea. I want to work on a resolution to submit to the mayor's office and use my report to document the process."

"Intriguing," Mrs. Achebe said. "What do you want to propose in your resolution?"

"It's about gun violence," Patrice said. "I think the police department needs to be held to account for every shooting in the city. 'Cause they obviously don't treat every case the same, and they should."

I could see where this was going, and I knew it was going to turn into something if I didn't keep my mouth shut. So I just stared at my desk, trying to think about something else.

"This is a very timely subject," Mrs. Achebe said. "Go on."

"I've been reading about this stuff since what happened to Zoe Knight," Patrice said. "A lot of people are really mad because the police aren't working on Zoe's case. And everyone knows the police don't care about Black people in this city."

There it was. I pulled my lips in and bit down hard.

"I heard they already closed the file on this one," Eddie said.

"I believe it," Patrice told him.

"Patrice, we're not going to peddle in rumors here," Mrs. Achebe said. "This is a journalism assignment. You need to back up anything you put in there with research and facts. Are you down for that?"

"Definitely," she said. "I already know that seventy-eight percent of gunshot victims in Washington are Black, and that the investigation rate is crazy low. *That's* a fact."

"The case closure rate is low," I said, before I even knew it was going to come out. "Not the investigation rate. There's a difference."

Everyone turned to look at me. They already knew Patrice and I had some friction about this stuff.

"Ali, don't even," she said, like I couldn't possibly know what I was talking about.

Eddie Cruz jumped in next, because I guess he

couldn't stand *not* being an idiot for one more minute, either.

"So then why aren't they even trying to solve Zoe's case?" he asked.

"They *are*," I said.

"Yeah," Eddie said. "Just like they 'investigate' all the others. Right before they bury it and forget about it."

I was feeling more heated by the second. And not because they were wrong about everything. They were just wrong about Zoe.

And in a way, they were wrong about me, too.

"You don't know anything about it!" I said. "You don't even know any real police!"

"Ali, calm down," Mrs. Achebe said.

I didn't want to calm down. I wanted to flip my desk and walk out of there. But I couldn't afford a trip to the principal's office right now. It was almost three-thirty, and when that bell rang, I had somewhere much more important to be.

"Ali, no offense, but you're just like the same song, playing over and over," Patrice said. "Black folks have all kinds of reasons not to trust the cops, and you're acting like just 'cause your dad works for the department—"

That's when I exploded.

"You think I'm stupid?" I said. "You think my dad hasn't been pulled over by some White cop for no good reason? You think my sister doesn't get followed around stores all the time, like she's just there to shoplift? How many different ways do I have to say it? I get it. I'm not an idiot."

I could tell that Patrice, and Eddie, and probably some others were rolling their eyes at me. I had zero cred with them. I wished Gabe, or Cedric, or Mateo, or Ruby were there to stick up for me. Because I was sick of doing it for myself.

"All right," Mrs. Achebe said. "Everyone just take a breath. Right now."

So we did, literally. Mrs. A always means what she says. Even her shirt spoke the truth. It said, BLACK HISTORY DIDN'T START WITH SLAVERY. Mrs. Achebe is always teaching with everything she's got.

"This is an important conversation," she said. "But I'm not going to let it turn into a shouting match. Patrice, you're more than welcome to write about this issue, as long as you stick to the facts. And it's not going to be about Zoe Knight, either. That's not your story to tell."

I was glad she said that last part, at least. Then, before anyone could get in a final word, the bell rang, and the school day was over.

I picked up my stuff and bolted.

"Ali?" I heard Mrs. Achebe calling after me. *"Ali? I'm not done talking to you."*

But I was already gone.

# CHAPTER 19

ONCE I'D BLASTED out of social studies, I ran down the hall, down two flights of stairs, and out the front of Washington Latin. I needed to be one of the first people outside, so I could take up a position across the street without anyone noticing.

By the time most of the school was pouring out through the main doors, I was on the top row of the playing field bleachers, watching out for Zoe.

When I spotted her, she was coming out with Ruby and Adele Freeman. Even from a distance, I could tell Zoe wanted to get away. She kept looking up the street and nodding at whatever Adele was saying.

I texted Ruby real quick, and saw her look down at her phone.

**Where is Zoe going, do you know? Don't tell her I'm asking.**

Zoe and Adele were still talking, but Ruby looked around like she was trying to spot me. I ducked down. I didn't want to blow this now. And a second later, Ruby texted back.

**I don't know. WHERE ARE YOU?**

**More later,** was all I wrote back. By then, Zoe was heading out and fast-walking up toward Kentucky Avenue.

As soon as she turned the corner out of sight, I cut diagonally across the fields, scaled the fence, and dropped onto the sidewalk.

It took a second to spot Zoe, but then I saw her maybe fifty yards ahead. She had her Beats on, which helped. She was also moving with a purpose.

I'd never tailed anyone like this. I was nervous and excited. All I really knew was that I had to stick close enough so I wouldn't lose her, and far enough away so she wouldn't notice me.

By the time I was trailing Zoe across Lincoln Park, I was also officially into one of Nana Mama's red zones. It wasn't a bad neighborhood, but it *was* farther from home than that map of hers said I was allowed to go by myself.

Oh, well. Dad says when I get onto something important, I'm like a dog with a bone. And I definitely wasn't letting go of this one anytime soon.

After about fifteen minutes, Zoe stopped at Capitol Hill Supermarket on Massachusetts Avenue. I didn't know if this was where she'd been heading all along, or if she was just making a stop. The market was too small for me to follow her inside. All I could really do was wait there behind a parked truck and hope she came back out again.

And after ten long, tense minutes of waiting, she finally did.

She had two heavy-looking grocery bags now. Both of them were hanging on her good arm. It didn't seem to slow her down, though.

Just past Union Station, she turned right onto

First Street. Then she went a few more blocks and took another right, onto K Street.

It was ten after four by then, and I knew we had to be getting close. So I hurried up to First and K, then stopped to scope out the next block.

Sure enough, Zoe was right there.

It was an underpass, like a little one-block tunnel. Up above, the train tracks ran into and out of Union Station. Down here on street level, it was some kind of camp for people experiencing homelessness. There were tents on the wide sidewalks, with a row of huge steel and concrete columns up the middle of the street.

Some people were coming and going like regular pedestrians, but a lot of other people were hanging out, not going anywhere.

I saw a guy cooking on a camp stove, and a kid playing cards with his dad on a cardboard box. An older girl in a long sweater was sitting on a milk crate and looking at her phone. A lot of the tents had words spray-painted on their sides, too.

OCCUPIED!

PLEASE DO NOT REMOVE

I'd heard about these camps, but I didn't know much about them. The people I saw experiencing homelessness every day were always out on the street. At least these folks had a roof over their heads, I guess.

Not that it was much.

Zoe was talking to an old lady by her tent. She'd set down her bags and was handing the lady a wrapped sandwich and a bottle of water.

"God bless you, sweetheart," the lady said, and gave her a hug before Zoe moved on down the row.

The only place for me to keep watching without getting spotted was from the other side of those columns down the middle of the underpass. I waited until Zoe wasn't looking, and scooted halfway across the street. Then I ducked in behind the barrier that kept cars from hitting the columns. I'd be safe there.

Safe enough, anyway.

I watched while Zoe worked her way along the sidewalk. The girl in the long sweater said something as she went by, but Zoe ignored her. She wasn't stopping to feed everyone. She would have needed ten more bags for that. But she did seem to know a lot of people.

And I'd finally figured out what was going on. It was something I should have realized a lot sooner.

When Zoe got to the last tent, a man with a beard, a camo jacket, and a Nationals hat was waiting for her. He gave her a big hug first, and then stared at her cast for a long time, talking to her. It was like he didn't even notice that big bag of food she'd brought.

I couldn't hear anything they were saying, but I knew exactly what I was seeing now.

I'd just found out where Zoe's dad lived.

# CHAPTER 20

IT WAS LIKE this did and didn't make sense at the same time. Zoe's mom was basically famous. The two of them lived in a nice house on C Street.

And her dad was experiencing homelessness?

Yeah. That's exactly what was going on.

Was she protecting him? Was he protecting her? And, same question as before—did any of this have anything to do with the other secrets Zoe was sitting on?

I still had no freaking clue.

Zoe didn't stay long, either. They sat on a couple of lawn chairs for a while, and he ate one of the sandwiches she'd brought him.

When he was done eating, they stood up again, and she hugged him for a long time. He kissed the top of her head, and waved good-bye as she walked away.

I pulled back, all the way behind the column where I'd been hiding. Then I gave it a slow ten count to let Zoe get ahead of me. After that, I was just about to move out, when I heard someone yell Zoe's name.

"Yo, Zoe! Wait up!"

I looked out again. It was the girl in the long sweater. Zoe wasn't slowing down for her though, any more than she did before. She just kept going around the corner onto First Street, while the other girl ran to catch up.

Normally, I would have stayed put for another ten count, at least, to keep myself off Zoe's radar. Except I'd just seen something that changed everything. It was what that other girl had on her feet. Heavy black boots, military style.

I couldn't swear they were the same black boots I'd seen on whoever had been standing next to Zoe after she got shot that day. Maybe they were and maybe they weren't. But right now, *maybe* was plenty enough to get me moving, quick.

I held up my hand to stop a car on its way through the tunnel. The guy blared his horn, but that was the least of my worries. I sprinted across the street, onto the sidewalk, and around the corner.

"Zoe!" I yelled, louder than I had to.

They'd already stopped. It looked like this girl was standing in the way, trying to keep Zoe from leaving. As I came up on them, she looked at me like I was nuts.

"Ali? What are you doing here?" Zoe asked.

"Kind of a long story," I said. "You okay?"

"Who's this?" the other girl said, but I ignored her.

"I'm walking home," I told Zoe. "You want to walk with me?"

I saw a lot of different things in Zoe's eyes then. Like confusion. And anger. But also maybe some relief.

"We're having a private conversation here, brother," the girl said. "Why don't you take your little security detail and wait over there?"

I wasn't going anywhere, though. Not without Zoe. This girl looked maybe seventeen. And I wasn't sure why she had her hand in her pocket, but I also wasn't sure I wanted to know. Mostly, I just wanted out of there.

Zoe ignored her, too.

"Yeah, I'm coming," she said. "Later, Mikayla."

The tall girl, Mikayla, stepped up on me as I walked by. I just kept moving with my chin up and my heart pounding until Zoe and I were out of there. We walked up First Street together and didn't look back.

I was relieved for sure, but at the same time, you could just *feel* the silence coming off of Zoe. I knew I wasn't off the hot seat yet.

Because I still had a lot of explaining to do.

# CHAPTER 21

WE GOT ABOUT a block away from Mikayla before Zoe stopped and got right up in my face.

"What are you doing here, Ali?" she asked. I felt like some cockroach she'd just turned on the light and found where he wasn't supposed to be.

"I'm sorry," I said. "I was just..."

"Just *what*?" she asked. It was hard to get stared at like that and think straight at the same time. My brain felt like one big glitch.

"Were you seriously following me?" Zoe asked.

"Yeah," I kind of mumbled out. "I was worried about you."

"You don't need to worry about me," she said. "I like you, Ali, but—"

"Actually, yeah, I do need to worry," I said.

"Excuse me?"

"Don't play me, Zoe," I said.

It was like something had just turned a corner in my mind. I wasn't going to tell her not to be mad. But at the same time, I was a little mad now, too.

And I kept going. "You want to pretend like everything's okay? Like you don't know who did this? That's up to you. But I *know* what I saw. And I know you're not telling me the truth."

"I don't want to hear it," she said.

She started walking again, but I went step for step with her. And I wasn't even trying to go easy about this anymore.

"I was right there, Zoe. I got your blood on me, and I won't ever forget that. I'm not saying you owe me anything. And I know you didn't ask for my help. But you can't stop me from caring about what happens to you. Not after all that."

I couldn't tell which way I was pushing my luck. I was still nervous Zoe would tell me to leave her alone, or start screaming at me. She even opened her mouth to say something, but then she stopped.

And then started again.

"I don't mean to yell at you," she said. "But Ali, you can't go around following people like this."

*Well, maybe,* I thought. *Detectives do it all the time, for really good reasons.*

"But also," Zoe went on. "Thank you."

"For what?" I asked.

"You know," she said. "For caring."

Then she did the most surprising thing of all. She leaned over and kissed me, right there on the sidewalk. And on the lips, too.

It would have been nicer if I'd seen it coming. The whole thing was like a blink, and over before I even knew it was happening.

But still, it was really nice. Like, one of the best things that's ever happened to me nice.

Zoe hooked her thumb up the block. "You want to keep moving?" she asked.

"Yeah," I said, and we walked on from there.

I had so many different things running around my head now, I didn't know what to say next. On the one hand, I didn't want to spoil what had just happened. But on the other hand, this was too important to let ride. Time's never on your side in an investigation.

And besides, keeping my mouth shut has never been one of my best skills.

"So listen," I said. "I don't want to make you mad all over again, but you should really know—I told my Dad what I saw in the park that day. Detective Matheson knows about it, too."

"Yeah," Zoe said. "I know."

"You do?" I asked. Man, this girl was full of surprises.

"They've been riding me about it," she said. "It's okay, though. I understand."

"Sorry," I said. "I know you hate the police—"

"Not because of all this," she said. "The thing I hate is how the cops never help the people who need it most. Especially Black folks. Every time you actually need some help, where are they? Nowhere, that's where. And then they turn around and go out of their way to make life even harder for people who don't deserve it. That's even worse."

I looked back toward the tent camp we'd left behind. "You mean people like..."

"Like my dad, yeah," she said. Then she pointed at a sign on the side of the street. "See that? That's exactly what I'm talking about right now."

It was a real metal sign, put up by the city. And now that I noticed, there were a lot of them up and down that block of First Street.

NOTICE
The District of Columbia government will conduct
a general cleanup of this area
on or after—

Below that part, it showed a handwritten date and time for about a week away. There was a lot of fine print, too, but I didn't read it all. I'd seen enough to understand.

"They do this all the time," Zoe said. "Cops come through those camps and take away everything.

People's tents. Their property. Their carts. They say you can come claim it at some garage, but most of the time they just throw it away. I mean, seriously, who does that to a person experiencing homelessness?"

"What will your dad do when they come?" I asked.

"Same as always. Find somewhere else to be, and then hopefully come back when he can."

It was like every answer just made room for more questions.

"How long as he been living…you know. Out here?" I asked.

"He doesn't want any help," Zoe said, like she'd seen right through to what I was *really* asking. "He's stubborn. Proud, too. He works at one of the soup kitchens, but it's not nearly enough."

"He has a job?"

"You'd be surprised," she said. "A lot of people in that camp have jobs. But do you know how expensive apartments are in DC? Minimum wage doesn't cut it."

"I guess," I said. It wasn't something I'd thought about much.

"Daddy says he'd rather live out here than get a handout from anyone, including my mom. He's kind of pigheaded, to keep it one hundred. But he's a good dad, I swear."

"That's really cold, what the city's doing," I said. "Is there any way I can help?"

Zoe shrugged. "You want to help? Talk to your father. Get him to do something about it."

"I will," I said. I didn't think there was much Dad could do, but I'd at least try.

And for whatever else it was worth, I'd just figured out what I wanted to write about for my big social studies report, too.

# CHAPTER 22

CEDRIC MET ME about a block from my house that Saturday morning and we walked over to Nubuilt Garage on E Street in Southwest.

Cedric said he'd take the lead on this one, and I let him. Maybe I knew more about this stuff, but his swag was at like three hundred compared to mine, in pretty much every way.

The idea was to scope out the garage first and see if we could tell whether Orlando was there. So when we hit that block of E Street, we hung back and just surveilled the place for a minute.

The garage was a little two-bay place with a Castrol sign hanging above the entrance. As far as I could tell, there were three people working that morning: a White guy in the first bay, fixing a car up on a lift, a Black lady in the office next to that, and an old Black man with a crown of gray hair, hanging out in the office, too.

Ruby had told us what Orlando looked like, and he definitely wasn't one of those three.

"Let's do this," Cedric said, and led the way over to that open garage door.

"Excuse me," Cedric tried, but the mechanic cut him off without even turning around.

"Nobody allowed in the bays, fellas," he said. "Talk to Monica."

He ticked his head to the side, where the lady was working at her computer, and the old guy was leaning against the counter, talking to her. So we stepped into the office and started again.

"Morning," Cedric said. "I was wondering if you could help me out?"

148

"Well, you don't look old enough to drive, sweet-heart," the lady said. "What can I do for *you*?"

"I'm twenty-two," Cedric said.

"No, you're not," the old guy said.

"Nah, I'm not," Cedric said. This was how he rolled. He always got people joking and relaxed before he tried to get anything out of them. In his own way, Cedric had some serious investigative skills. I wasn't even nervous.

"Actually, I'm looking for my cousin Orlando," Cedric told them.

"Why? He owe you some money?" the old guy asked. He and the lady cracked up at that, like Orlando was another whole kind of joke. Which maybe he was.

"I wish," Cedric said, playing along. "Nah, we cool, I just hadn't seen him in a minute. He works weekends, right?"

"Not usually," the lady said.

The old guy squinted at a clipboard on the wall, next to a calendar with a picture of a sexy lady on it. "Yeah, he's here Monday to Thursday," the guy said.

"So does that mean he definitely wasn't here last Saturday, either?" Cedric asked. "He told me this is when I could find him." It was a little genius move, just so we could make sure. Cedric was playing this perfectly.

"You either heard wrong, or Orlando don't want to see you," the man said, and they laughed again, like this was the funniest place to work in Washington. It wasn't what I was expecting, at all.

"Sorry, hon," the lady said. Then she held up a plate from her desk. "You boys want a snickerdoodle instead? Made them myself."

"No, thank you, ma'am," I said, but Cedric took one and stuck the whole thing in his mouth.

"Dang, these are awesome," he said, chowing down. And of course, now I wished I'd taken one, too. But we weren't there for cookies.

"Who should I tell Orlando was looking for him?" the lady asked, ducking her chin to see over the top of her glasses.

"Just tell him Loki says hi," Cedric said. "Come on, Cassius, let's get out of these nice people's way."

He even took two more cookies when they

weren't looking, and gave me one after we'd hit the street. I know everyone says I'm the detective, but I wish I had half of Cedric's moves.

"So, what now?" he asked, once we were out of earshot.

"Well, it doesn't necessarily mean Orlando *was* at Anacostia Park last week," I said. "But it's a step in the right direction."

"Okay. And?" Cedric asked. It was like he knew his part was over and now he was waiting for me to kick in with whatever I brought to the table.

"And," I told him, "I think it's safe to say we have our first real suspect."

# CHAPTER 23

ZOE LIVED IN a nice house on C Street between Ninth and Tenth in Southeast. I showed up that Saturday night with Gabe, Cedric, and Mateo. Ruby was already there, helping set up and everything.

"This is about the most awesome party I've ever been to," Gabe said, maybe ten seconds after we'd piled in the door.

There were people jamming in the living room. A giant dining room table was practically falling over with the mountain of food they'd put out. And either Dee-Cee, or Zoe, or Kim was some kind of plant freak, too. The whole house was green all over, including a huge rubber tree with little Christmas lights that hung above the front door when you walked in.

"It's *about* the most awesome party?" Mateo said. "Like you've ever been to something better?"

"Hey, hey, hey," Zoe said, coming over with Ruby. "Wassup, fellas? Thanks for coming."

"Thanks for inviting us," Gabe said.

"How you doing, Zoe?" Cedric asked.

"I'm good," she said. She seemed it, too, which was cool to see. I wasn't sure what to expect after the day before.

"Check the custom J's," Ruby said, pointing at Zoe's feet.

They were black with white skulls all over, like the opposite of those pink ones Zoe liked so much. Except somehow, they were totally her, too. And probably at least three hundred bucks.

"Sweet! Where'd you get those?" Cedric asked.

"They were a present from Darnell," she said. He was just walking by and gave her a little side hug on his way through.

"Nice present," Mateo said.

"Right?" Darnell said, with those diamond studs flashing in his ears, and another big rock in the football ring on his left hand. Something told me money wasn't one of Darnell's problems. "Wear them in good health, darling," he told her.

As he walked away, Zoe kind of lowered her voice. "I'm not going to say being in the hospital was any joke," she told us, "but I ain't mad about the lucre."

"Lucre," I said. "Good word."

"Girl's a poet," Ruby said, like we didn't already know. "Check it out."

She pointed at this huge cake in the middle of the dining room table. It had white icing, with a pair of blue and purple wings airbrushed on top. And in chocolate writing, it said—

I soar!
Every day,
Every minute,
Every breath.
Up, and up, and up,
Rising like Maya.
—ZK

"You wrote that?" I asked.

Zoe rolled her eyes. "It's so embarrassing," she said. "Dee-Cee can't help herself."

We hadn't been there very long, but Gabe was right. It was an awesome party, and we were already having a good time. The music was tight, and it kind of felt like we'd stepped into some bubble, away from everything else that had been going on for the last week.

"Zoe, baby! Come here!" Dee-Cee called out from over by the piano. But then she saw me, and stood up. "Oh, hey, Ali!"

"Hi, Ms. Knight!" I said.

*"Excuse me?"* she said, coming over with that giant smile of hers.

"I mean, hi, Dee-Cee," I said, while Gabe stood there looking starstruck.

"That's more like it," she said, and gave everyone hugs all around. "You boys make sure to stuff your faces, okay? Momma don't do leftovers."

"Yes ma'am," Cedric said. We'd heard about Dee-Cee's cooking and we'd all skipped lunch on purpose.

A second later, Dee-Cee was headed back to the piano, and the Ali Cross detective agency was headed for its next big mission—to make sure the dining room table didn't collapse under all that cake, roast chicken, ham, greens, corn bread, beans, and mac and cheese, and I didn't even know what else.

But we were definitely going to find out.

# CHAPTER 24

"So you live here with your mom and your aunt?" I asked Zoe a little later. We were both sitting with plates on our laps, stuffing our faces like we'd been told to do.

"Yeah." Zoe pointed her fork at the swinging door to the kitchen, where Kim was just coming out with a pitcher of iced tea.

"Hey, Z," she said. "How you hanging in?"

"I'm good," Zoe said. "Aunt Kim, this is Ali. You guys met at the—"

"Hospital," she said, and put down the pitcher. "Yes, hello again. Nice to see you."

She didn't wear a lot of makeup and jewelry like Dee-Cee. She had a short afro, and her clothes were simple—just a white T-shirt and jeans, with bare feet. I never would have guessed she was Dee-Cee's sister, but I was mentally writing it all down for later. So far, Kim was the biggest question mark on my persons-of-interest list.

"Ali, can I get you something to drink?" she asked.

"No, thank you, ma'am," I said. "I'll grab something."

She kind of looked twice at me, and smiled. "Ma'am," she said. "That's cute. I like it." But she didn't tell me to call her Kim.

"Hey, Kay-Kay?" Darnell said from the kitchen, and waved at her to come that way, which she did.

"Yeah, so anyway," Zoe said, "Aunt Kim's like my backup mom, when Dee-Cee's on the road. She's where I got my middle name, too."

That made sense. I'd been wondering what that K stood for.

"Cool," I said. "Does your mom tour a lot?"

"Just depends," Zoe said. "Lately, there's been a lot of work, so yeah. She's trying to get an agent in LA."

I hoped that didn't mean they were going to move away, but I didn't say so.

"Listen," I said, after another bite of mac and cheese, "I was wondering if it would be okay with you if I wrote about what the city's doing to that tent camp over on K Street."

Zoe looked like she liked that idea right away.

"You'd do that?" she asked.

I shrugged. "I've got to have a topic by Monday," I said, and she punched me in the arm. "I'm kidding," I said. "Yeah. It seems like a really important thing to write about."

"It is," she said. "You should come back there with me."

"What about Mikayla?" I asked.

"Don't worry about her," Zoe told me, even though she didn't explain. "I told my dad I'd help him get his stuff ready to go before the cops come for that next sweep. What do you think?"

I wasn't positive I could pull it off, Nana-wise,

and Dad-wise, but what was I going to say? *No, sorry, I didn't mean it?* Besides, that was exactly the kind of "primary source" research Mrs. Achebe was always pushing us to do.

"Sure," I said. "That'd be cool."

"I'll text you," she said, and wrapped her foot around my ankle for a second, and smiled right into my eyes. I could have sat there like that all night, but it was over just as quick as our first kiss.

"Zoe!" Dee-Cee yelled out from the piano. "Come sit with me, baby!"

Zoe took a deep breath and stood up. "I guess it's showtime," she said.

I didn't know what was happening, but I followed her into the living room, where Dee-Cee was clanging a spoon against her glass to get everyone's attention.

"Hey, y'all," she said. "Thank you so much for coming, and for helping me share the joy in having my girl home from the hospital."

Everyone cheered for that, and Zoe put her fists up, like a prizefighter, pink cast and all, which got a good laugh.

"Also, thank you to my beautiful sister, Kim, for minding the kitchen all night while I'm out here with you people," Dee-Cee said.

She motioned to the back of the room, where Kim was leaning in the archway to the dining room. Everyone cheered for her, too, but she didn't even smile. She seemed kind of unhappy, actually, and I wondered what it was like to have Dee-Cee Knight for a sister.

But everyone's eyes were back on Dee-Cee the next second.

"We're going to start off nice and easy here," she said, and turned to the guy on drums in the corner. Then she spit out a baseline rhythm, and he picked it up from there. Another lady had an electric guitar, and she started riffing on top of that, while Dee-Cee sat down at the keyboard to add her own thing to the mix.

It got even better from there. Dee-Cee sang some song I didn't know, but just about everyone else seemed to. They were all singing along, and dancing, and still cheering, while I stood there thinking about how much my dad would have loved this. He plays piano, too, and listens to music every chance he gets.

When it was over, and everyone was cheering their heads off all over again, I looked around, just taking in the room.

And the only person who wasn't clapping, or yelling, or even smiling, was Kim. She hadn't moved from her spot the whole time, as far as I could tell. Not until I caught her eye. Then she turned away and slipped back into the kitchen like this was no party at all for her.

Which, for all I knew anymore, it wasn't.

# CHAPTER 25

LATER THAT NIGHT, I was hanging out on the stairs with Gabe, Cedric, and Mateo, just yapping and arguing about the best superhero movie franchise. Like we do. It's *Avengers*, obviously, but try telling that to Cedric. He was mouthing off about *Dr. Strange* and cracking us up with his crazy opinions, when Ruby caught my eye.

Everyone else was in the living room, talking and listening to Dee-Cee play. But Ruby was standing alone in the dining room. Something about the way she looked at me said, *come here, right now.*

"Be right back," I told the fellas and walked over. She was at the end of the food table closest to the kitchen, holding an empty plate like she was getting ready to load up again.

"Are you seriously still hungry?" I asked, but she cut me off.

"*Shh!* Something's going on," she whispered.

So I shut up and listened. Sure enough, there were voices coming from the kitchen. I couldn't hear all of what they were saying, but you could tell they were getting heated about something in there.

"...don't lecture me..." someone said. It sounded like Kim.

And then Darnell. "If Dee-Cee finds out about this—"

"She's not going to find out!"

"She will if the cops know."

*The cops?* That last part jumped right out at me. Ruby, too. She was eyeballing me now like, *see?* She also started putting carrots and dip on her plate, almost in slow motion, just trying to look like we had some reason for standing there. Because something was definitely going on.

"Back off, Darnell. This is none of your business—"

"Keep your voice down!"

"Excuse me? Last I checked, I don't work for you."

"Come back here!"

The kitchen door swung open, and Kim walked right by us. Then she went straight over to Dee-Cee at the piano, leaned down, and whispered in her ear.

I couldn't read anything on Dee-Cee's face. She just nodded and kept playing without missing a note. Zoe was on the piano bench next to her mom, and she was watching it all happen, the same as us. When she saw me, she smiled like nothing was wrong, but I wasn't so sure.

Kim didn't wait around, either. She went from the piano to the front door, took a jacket off one of the hooks, and left.

"What was all that?" Ruby asked.

"Wish I knew," I said.

Before I could think about it anymore, a loud

crash came from the kitchen behind us. It sounded like breaking dishes or glass.

The music stopped, and everyone looked in our direction. Then the kitchen door opened again and Darnell stuck his head out.

"My bad!" he said. He was smiling, but I noticed he was breathing hard, too, like he was still worked up.

"That's coming out of your next check!" Dee-Cee yelled back, and everyone laughed, before Darnell ducked out again and the party went back to normal.

This seemed like a chance to do a little digging, if I made it quick.

"I'm going to go in there and help clean up," I told Ruby. She nodded because she knew exactly what I meant.

"Maybe I'll go get a little fresh air," she said. And I knew what she meant, too.

So while Ruby went outside to see which way Kim had gone, I pushed through that kitchen door to see what I could find out about Darnell.

He was pulling a broom and dustpan out of a

closet when I came in. There was a bunch of broken pieces on the floor, and a big food stain splattered on the wall.

"Hey, little man," he said. His smile still looked forced to me.

"You need a hand?" I asked.

My heart was kicking the whole time. I wasn't afraid of Darnell, exactly, but he was a big dude. It didn't take a lot of imagination to think about what else he could do if he got mad enough.

"I'm good," he said. "Just dropped a plate."

I wasn't buying it, though. That stain on the wall looked a lot to me like someone had *thrown* a plate, not dropped it. So I tried to keep the conversation going.

"Hey, those are some dope Jordans you got for Zoe," I said. "Where'd you pick those up?" Mostly, I wanted to see if Darnell responded to Zoe's name. If she was already on his mind, it might show on his face somehow.

But he didn't even answer.

"You sure you don't need some help?" I tried again.

"Why don't you go back out there and enjoy yourself?" Darnell asked.

It wasn't like a question, though. More like an order. I didn't have the spine to push it any further, so I headed out like he wanted me to, while my mind ran, and ran, and ran.

I had about eighteen different questions poking at me now. Most of all, I wondered if that argument had anything to do with Zoe. Maybe it was about something else completely, but they *had* mentioned the cops. I felt like I had some good reasons to be curious.

And either way, it sure seemed like every time I turned around, there was another secret coming out of that house. Now, more than ever, I wanted to know why.

# CHAPTER 26

THERE WASN'T ANY chance to update the guys at the party. Instead, I texted them when I got home and we all met online. Ruby was spending the night at Zoe's. She was going to report back later. Meanwhile, I told Gabe, Cedric, and Mateo about everything we'd seen and heard.

"You think it had anything to do with Zoe?" Gabe asked.

"That's exactly what I've been wondering," I said. "I couldn't get a read on Darnell, and I'm still

169

waiting to hear from Ruby about what's up with Kim."

"Long as we're talking, what about Orlando Fletcher?" Cedric asked. "Isn't he the one we should be focusing on, anyway?"

"Yeah, but I just don't know how," I said. "It's not like we can do real surveillance."

"Actually," Gabe said, "I set up some Google Alerts on him, and I've been watching his Instagram."

"Seriously?" Cedric said.

Gabe was way more low-key about his skills than he needed to be. But that only made it cooler when he pulled out something like this on his own.

"Orlando doesn't have any other socials, as far as I can tell, but I did get his home address," he said. "So I guess you could say we *are* surveilling him."

"That's all legal, right?" Mateo asked.

"I'm just surfing the web," Gabe answered. "No harm, no foul."

"Nice," Cedric said. "So what happens next?"

"We wait to hear if Ruby got anything on Kim or Darnell," I said. "And maybe we can find a way to put some real eyes on Orlando, too."

"Somehow," Gabe said.

"That sounds like a *me* kinda thing," Cedric said. "Mateo can back me up."

"I can?" Mateo asked.

"Yeah."

This whole investigation was turning out to be way more complicated than I ever thought it would get. It was all still just a bunch of puzzle pieces, and I couldn't even figure out which ones belonged, and which were part of something else.

The weirdest thing, though, was Zoe herself. She was the one who could tell us who had done this to her. But something was obviously keeping her from it.

And that *something* was the core of everything else. That's what my gut told me. It was the biggest blank we still had to fill.

The good news was, I like puzzles, and I tend to be good at them once I get started.

The bad news? Something told me I wasn't going to be getting a whole lot of sleep that night.

# CHAPTER 27

RUBY: YOU AWAKE?

ALI: Yeah. Can't sleep.

RUBY: I thought so. Thinking about Zoe and all that?

ALI: I was. Now I'm working on my social studies report, like the geek I am. Hello, Saturday night. Still can't sleep.

RUBY: Hey, whatever it takes:-)

ALI: Lol...what's up? You find anything out?

RUBY: Kim never came home. I even texted her to see if she was okay, but she didn't answer.

ALI: Maybe she has a boyfriend or something?

RUBY: If she has a boyfriend, that's news to me.

ALI: Where are you?

RUBY: Zoe's room. She's out cold.

ALI: What about Darnell? You get anything after we left?

RUBY: Nope. He went home around twelve. Never said anything about Kim as far as I know.

ALI: Keep me posted, ok?

RUBY: For sure

ALI: Thx

RUBY: What are you doing for your report, anyway?

ALI: Something about homelessness. What about you?

RUBY: I was going to do a profile on Dee-Cee, but then the whole shooting happened and I thought maybe not. But now maybe it's okay to jump back in ... ??

ALI: It might be good, if you know what I mean. See where Dee-Cee's head is at.

RUBY: I'll see what I can do. Catch you later.

ALI: Hey one other thing. Did Z ever say anything to you about her dad since this all started up?

RUBY: Nothing. Why?

ALI: Just curious. Later! Get some sleep ...

RUBY: Look who's talking.

ALI::-)

**ALEX CROSS ROLLED** Ali out of bed just after ten o'clock that Sunday morning. It was a good hour later than Ali usually got up on weekends, but he looked exhausted all the same.

"You all right?" Alex asked.

"Just up late," Ali said. Still, he perked up fast enough once he heard where they were going.

The father-and-son day Alex had planned began with a late breakfast at their favorite spot, Armando's. Ali ordered his usual, a tall stack slathered in berries, maple syrup, and whipped cream, with thick-cut bacon on the side. A less-than-healthy meal once in a while wasn't going to hurt anyone, especially without Nana there to see what the boy was scarfing down.

After that, they walked over to Nationals Stadium to see the Nats take on the Phillies. Now that the hometown team had added World Series Champs to their résumé, attendance was way up, with a capacity crowd of eighty-two thousand expected that afternoon.

Just outside the stadium, they passed a man in a ratty coat, mismatched shoes, and no socks, kneeling on the sidewalk with a cardboard sign.

HUNGRY. ANYTHING HELPS.

"Dad, can I have a dollar?" Ali asked.

Alex gave him a five instead. "Now you, too," he told his son, and Ali coughed up a dollar of his own.

As they made their way inside and over to section 132, just off the first base line, Ali was mostly quiet. Something had obviously taken root in his mind. Alex suspected it had something to do with the panhandler.

And then, sure enough, just after they got to their seats, he spoke up again.

"Hey, Dad? Do you know anything about those homeless camps around the city?" he asked.

"I know they've been controversial," Alex said. "Especially these so-called cleanups they've been doing. Why do you ask?"

"I think I'm going to write something about it for my social studies project," he said.

"Good topic. How'd you land on that?"

Ali paused, and shrugged. "I don't know. I heard some people talking about it at school, and it just kind of stuck, I guess. I was wondering if I could interview you about it."

"Happy to do what I can," he told Ali. "But just so you know, the police are only on-site for those cleanups as a security detail. It's the Office of Health and Human Services who really call the shots there."

Ali pulled out his phone and punched in a note to himself. "So there's nothing the police department can do about how they run those things?" he asked.

"Other than being respectful and keeping the peace, no," Alex told him. "I can help you get in touch with HHS, if you want to start there. I'm sure somebody will talk to you."

Ali went quiet again after that, and the game got underway. Stephen Strasburg threw a quick strike-out, but then gave up a single to the Phillies' Bryce Harper.

Even then, Ali barely responded to the play. His mind was clearly somewhere else. "Hey, Dad?"

"Yeah?"

"Do you know if they have anything new on Zoe's case?" he asked.

That was the question Alex had been expecting all morning. He took his time now, and thought through what he knew about the investigation.

Dee-Cee Knight had been cleared of any suspicion. Orlando Fletcher was clearly at the top of Detective Matheson's suspect list. But none of that was public information, even if Ali did have some personal involvement.

"You know there's a lot I can't tell you," Alex explained. "But do you have any specific questions?"

"Well, yeah," Ali said. "Do they know if Detective Matheson has any suspects?"

"I think he does," Alex said, without going into any detail. "But now I'm curious. What do *you* think? You're the closest thing they've got to an eyewitness."

Ali seemed to ponder the question, ignoring the game for another several seconds. "I don't think it was a random thing," he said. "I think the shooter was probably someone Zoe knows."

It was impressive how often Ali could read a situation and come to the same conclusion that Alex had. The boy's constantly running mind made him a natural investigator—for better or worse. It also made him something of a worrier.

Ali took a deep breath then, like he was making way for what had really been on his mind all along.

"It just seems like I keep hearing people hating on the cops and saying how none of them care about Zoe's case," Ali said. "And I know that's not true. I mean, I get it. I know there's a lot of bad stuff police do all the time, but whenever I try to tell someone there's more to it than that, it's like they don't want to listen."

"People are angry for a lot of good reasons," Alex said. "For some of them, it doesn't matter if there's more to the story. Not in the case of actual police brutality, or other mistreatment. But you know that, too."

"That's what I try to tell them at school," Ali said. "I get it. This is complicated. But just because I'm a cop's kid doesn't mean I can't see straight about it all."

Down on the field, a sudden double play turned the top of the inning into the bottom, and the game moved on.

Alex tried to move on, as well.

"Speaking of Zoe, are you two a thing now?" he asked.

"Nah," Ali said, almost immediately. It was about as convincing as a cat with canary feathers coming out of his mouth.

"Well, if you ever need advice on girl stuff—"

"Dad..."

"Okay, okay."

In some ways, Ali had always been an open book and easy to read. But these days, he was showing a more private side, like a lot of kids his age. It was as though Ali had moved half into shadow, and the details of his life were getting harder to see, for Alex.

So it was difficult not to give the subject just one more try.

"She seems like a great girl, anyway," Alex said. "But then again, what do I know? I'm a thousand years old. Girls hadn't been invented when I was in middle school."

Ali shrugged back impatiently, even as a smile seemed to fight its way onto his face. Apparently, there was only so much he could keep inside. It was nice, like watching the sun come out.

"Thanks, Dad," he said. "And yeah, she really is kind of awesome."

Now it was Alex's turn to smile. This was turning out to be a great day, after all.

# CHAPTER 28

**THAT WEDNESDAY MORNING,** I was coming out of math when I saw Zoe standing there waiting for me.

"Wassup?" she said. "You get my text?"

I guess she used her phone in school a lot more than I did. I usually played by the rules and kept mine off, at least during class.

"Not yet," I said, and she motioned at me to follow her around the corner, away from everyone else. Truthfully? I thought we were about to kiss again. But that's not how it went.

"You still want to help?" she asked. "Because that sweep is happening over on K Street today."

"Oh...that," I said, catching up.

"What'd you think I was going to say?"

"Nothing," I told her. "Anyway, yeah. I can help."

"Awesome. Meet me over in front of that CVS on the corner in like five minutes," she said. "I don't think we should try and leave together. I'll go through the cafeteria, okay?"

"Um..." I said.

Up until then, I'd thought she was talking about going after school, which was risky enough. But now I realized she was talking about *skipping* school. And that was a whole other thing.

I'd ditched a couple classes before, but I'd never left the building like this, in the middle of the day. Five minutes from now, I was supposed to be in English, giving my oral report on *New Kid*. It's an awesome book, and I actually wanted to be there for it.

But meanwhile, I'd already told Zoe I'd do it, and the fact was, I *wanted* to. Not just to impress her. I really did want to help.

"Ali?" she asked, waving a hand in front of my face.

"Sorry. Yeah, I'll see you out there in five," I said, and we split up.

I hustled straight down the stairs, covering as much ground as I could before the fourth period bell. That's when the halls would clear out, and I wanted to be gone by then.

Pretty soon, I was on the covered walkway behind the building, where they had some trailers set up as temporary classrooms. Behind that was a fence with a gate we weren't supposed to use, but the gate chain was long enough that someone my size could squeeze through. Kids did it all the time.

So just as I heard that fourth period bell from inside the school, I was sliding out to the sidewalk on Thirteenth Street.

I kept moving, too. It was still possible someone might spot me, so I put my head down and sprinted over to meet Zoe around the corner. She was exactly where she said she'd be when I got there.

"I called an Uber," she told me. "Two minutes."

I'm not allowed to have Uber on my phone, or

even a credit card, but I guess that's how it rolled in Zoe's world.

"Does your mom know you're doing this?" I asked.

"She knows I see my dad sometimes," she said. "But I don't tell her every time I go."

Which I guess was a no. At least we were in the same boat that way.

A minute later, the car pulled up. We got in, took off, and I reached over to hold her hand in the backseat. Which she let me do. It was nice.

"Thanks for coming," she said. "I appreciate it."

I had a ton of questions about what to expect, and what we were actually going to be doing when we got there, but I didn't want to sound all needy about it.

Meanwhile, I was wondering if Mrs. Gordon would let me make up my book report, and if I was going to get a detention for skipping.

I was also thinking about everything I'd seen at that camp on K Street the last time. And about everything that had happened there, too.

"Do you think that girl Mikayla is going to be

around?" I asked. Mikayla was the one part I was most nervous about. I didn't want any trouble, and she seemed like the type to go looking for it.

"Don't worry about Mikayla. It'll be fine," Zoe told me. Which was easy for her to say. She wasn't afraid of anything, as far as I could tell. "We're just going to help some people get packed up and out of there. Don't overthink it," she said.

"See, but overthinking's my specialty," I said. It got a laugh, and made me feel a little bit less nervous.

Not that it mattered anymore. Because unless I was ready to jump out of a moving Uber, there was no turning back now.

# CHAPTER 29

WE MADE A quick stop on the way, at a food truck Zoe knew about. They sold something called Bread-coin, which we were going to give to people at the camp. Each one was worth $2.20 at a bunch of different places all over the city where you could get food. Zoe bought a whole pocketful of them.

"People gonna be too busy this morning," she said. "This way they can pick something up for themselves later."

She really did care, and not just about her dad, I

could tell. Other than skipping school, I felt like I was doing a good thing, in a lot of ways.

When we got to the underpass on K Street, everything was different than before. A lot more people were around, breaking down tents and packing their things into shopping carts, bags, and boxes.

At the end of the row, Zoe's dad already had his tent down. Zoe ran over and gave him a hello hug.

"Daddy, this is Ali. We're here to help," she told him.

"You shouldn't be here, T-bird," he said. "The two of you ought to be in school."

"This *is* for school. Ali's writing a report," she said.

Mr. Knight just gave Zoe a look.

"Well, we're here now," she said. "What do you need?"

He smiled then, and you could tell he was glad she was there. "Hold that bag open for me, please," he said, and pointed at his big duffel.

Even with the cast on her arm, Zoe was able to

help him start packing away his tent and get ready to go.

"So you're writing a report?" Mr. Knight asked.

"Yes, sir."

"What's your angle?"

"Excuse me?"

"Daddy used to write," Zoe said. "That's how he and Momma met. He reviewed one of her shows for *Rolling Stone*."

"What's *Rolling Stone*?" I asked, and Mr. Knight looked at Zoe like, *Where'd you get this guy?*

"Only the greatest music publication of all time," he said.

"You should look him up," Zoe said. "His pen name was—"

"Cameron Thompson," Mr. Knight said. "I fancied myself a novelist back then, and thought I'd save my real name for that."

Which explained a lot, I realized. That's why Stephen Knight hadn't shown up on Gabe's web searches.

Zoe had already told me that her dad had a job, but I only knew that he worked at a soup kitchen.

188

It sounded like he'd had a whole other career, too. Until he didn't. I wondered how he got from there to here, but I didn't want to be all nosy about it. I was learning plenty, just by being there.

Even Mrs. Achebe would have approved. Not about the skipping out part, but this was exactly the kind of hands-on research we were supposed to include for our reports. It couldn't just be stuff we got off the web.

"What should I do?" I asked.

Mr. Knight pointed toward the other end of the tunnel. "Go see if Elizabeth needs anything," he told Zoe. "I'm in good shape."

So we walked back up the row, and gave out those Breadcoins along the way. Zoe answered some questions for me, too.

"Where are they all going to go?" I asked.

"Wherever they can," she said. "That's why a lot of these camps are near train and bus stations."

It was all so complicated. I couldn't imagine living on the street and trying to manage all my stuff that way, making sure nobody took anything, and trying to have a job, all at the same time.

I mean, I'd always known there were people experiencing homelessness, obviously. I see them almost every day in my neighborhood. But now it all seemed way more real.

"What about stuff like bathrooms?" I asked. "Where do they go? Or is that a stupid question?"

Zoe didn't mind, though.

"Wherever they can," she said. "Union Station, or...well, to be honest, you probably don't want to know. And you can't keep a lot of food sitting around, either, because the rats come after it. Either real ones, or the human kind."

"People don't watch out for each other down here?" I asked.

"Some do," Zoe said. Which obviously meant that some didn't.

The good news was I hadn't seen Mikayla around. Maybe she'd already packed up and gone. It was hard to know, because some of the carts and boxes looked like they'd been left behind. Or else people were just finding a spot first and then coming back for them. I wasn't sure.

Eventually, we got down to the old lady from the other day. The one Zoe had brought a sandwich to. She had her own tent and some stuff in a big box sitting next to a little rolling cart on the sidewalk.

"Elizabeth, this is my friend, Ali," she said. "He can give you a hand if you want."

"Oh, bless you," she said. "This box is way too heavy for me."

I wondered what she did when she was on her own. She wasn't as old as Nana Mama, but that's who I thought about. If I knew my great-grandma was living on the street and struggling to get by like this, it would break my heart in a million places.

"Where are you going to take your stuff now?" I asked, getting that box into the cart for her.

"Tonight, I'll probably just keep moving," she said. "I'll see if I can't come back here tomorrow."

"You can't sleep in a shelter?" I asked.

Elizabeth shook her head. "Depends on the shelter. Last time I slept inside, someone took my good shoes and all they left me were these."

I'd already noticed the ratty old high-tops she

was wearing. The sole on one was flopping around and I could see her toes on the other foot. The whole thing made me really sad. Mad, too. Nobody deserved to live this way.

And it was all about to get worse.

A *lot* worse.

# CHAPTER 30

JUST WHEN I was helping Elizabeth get the last of her stuff jammed into that cart, she looked at something over my shoulder and pressed her mouth shut tight.

"Mm-hm. Here we go," she said.

Two city trucks had just pulled over on the side of the underpass. Some people in green coveralls got out and started putting orange cones along the lane of traffic closest to the sidewalk. A second crew was doing the same thing on the other side of the street, where there was another row of tents and people packing up.

A couple of cop cars had rolled in, too, and parked at either end of the tunnel. I could see some officers stationing themselves outside their cruisers. For security, I guess. But I understood why the folks who camped here might not see it that way.

"You almost packed up?" one of the workers asked Elizabeth. "It's after eleven."

"Don't got much choice, do I?" Elizabeth said.

"No, ma'am," the guy told her. He wasn't being mean, but he wasn't exactly being nice, either.

Then I heard someone yelling. "Hey! That's mine!"

It was Mikayla, I saw. A worker had just grabbed one of the carts that had been sitting off to the side and he was dumping all the stuff into the back of his truck. Maybe Mikayla had gone off to find a new spot, I don't know, but now she was back for it. And it looked like she was too late. I felt sorry for her, actually.

"Calm down," one of the guys in coveralls said.

"*You* try calming down when I take that truck of yours," Mikayla told him.

People were coming over to see what was going on.

"Mikayla?" Elizabeth asked. "What's up here?"

"These people think they can take my stuff—"

"Technically, we can," the guy said. "You've all been duly warned—"

Mikayla threw a bunch of curse words at him, and climbed onto the back bumper of his truck to reach inside.

"Hey!" He grabbed her by the arm.

"Get off me!" she yelled at him.

"Just get down here!"

"Quit it!" I told him.

I didn't stop to think like I probably should have. I stepped in to help, if I could. I'm not even sure what I was trying to do, but I got caught in the scuffle. The guy yanked Mikayla back onto the side-walk, and she slammed into me just as I got there.

I went down hard. My mouth hit the cement, and I tasted blood.

"Ali!" Zoe said, and came over as I sat up. When

I ran my tongue over my front teeth, I could feel a sharp edge where one of them had broken.

"Ali!" Zoe said again. "You're hurt!" She was kneeling next to me now, while the fight with Mikayla and the maintenance guy kept going on. They were shouting at each other, and practically on top of me. Mikayla was crying, too.

"Give me that!" she said, and reached right over me to grab a handful of clothes back from the guy.

That's when I saw the gun. It was inside Mikayla's sweater and tucked into her waist at the back. The pistol had a squared-off stock, and looked to me like a 9mm. I don't like guns, but 9mm are standard issue for the police department. I know one when I see one.

Nine millimeter was also the caliber of weapon that had been used on Zoe at Anacostia Park that day.

"Ali, are you okay?" Zoe asked me again.

It was all going by in a blur. The cops were coming over now. My jaw hurt like crazy. My lip was bleeding.

But mostly, I was thinking about that pistol. And

those black boots Mikayla was still wearing. And that long sweater of hers, the one that I might have mistaken for a coat when I saw *someone* standing over Zoe right after she got shot.

Was Mikayla that person? Was she the shooter we'd been looking for?

All those feelings from that day at the park washed over me like some kind of nasty echo. I remembered seeing Zoe hurt. Not knowing what to do. Wondering if another shot was going to go off.

But that was then. This was now. I had to focus.

Two cops had come over, and both of them were arguing with Mikayla.

"I need them to stop taking my property," she said. "I didn't do nothing!"

"Miss, you need to calm down," one of the cops told her.

"I just need my cart," she said, pointing at the truck and trying to get to it. "It's right there."

"I don't know if that's yours," the second cop said. She'd put herself in Mikayla's way now and wasn't budging. "Just take a step back. This is your last warning. We *will* arrest you."

"Whatcha warning *her* for?" somebody called out.

"Just let her take her stuff and go!" Zoe said. "Leave her alone!"

"Everyone, give us some room!" the other cop shouted at the crowd. He turned and started forcing people to back up, even while I was still down there on one knee, bleeding from the mouth. But he didn't seem to care about that.

This was going from bad to worse, quick. And I knew what I had to do next. There was no question.

I just wished I didn't have to do it.

# Chapter 31

I STOOD UP to talk to the nearest cop, and when I did, I kept my voice low.

"Sir, I think the police might be looking for that girl," I said. "It's about a case that belongs to a guy named Detective Matheson at MPD."

"Oh, yeah?" he asked, like I was talking non-sense. If he cared that I was bleeding, he didn't say so. "How do you know that?"

"She's carrying a nine-millimeter weapon," I told

him. "And I think it might have been used in a shooting last week. My dad is with MPD, too."

"Your dad?"

"Detective Alex Cross," I said.

For the first time, the cop really looked at me. I could see right away how he'd flipped one-eighty and suddenly wondered if he ought to be taking me seriously. Zoe was trying to talk to the other cop, but everything was a crazy mess.

"Hey, Roberts," my cop said, and jerked his head in Mikayla's direction. "Pat her down, will you?"

I stood up to see better, but he grabbed me by the shoulder to stop me.

"What are you doing?" I asked.

"Taking you home," he said. "You shouldn't be here. And your mouth is a mess. You're going to need a dentist."

"But I just told you—"

"Exactly. It's not safe here."

I couldn't believe it. Now all of a sudden, he cared about my well-being? Just because of who my dad was? I couldn't say anything for sure, but it seemed like a pretty good guess.

And either way, he wasn't letting me get any closer to what was going on. I could only watch while the other cop, Roberts, put Mikayla up against the wall and started frisking her.

"Hey! *Hey!* There's no call for that!" someone said.

"Why you messing with her?" someone else said.

"Ali!" Zoe yelled. I thought she was still trying to help me, but when I saw her face, I realized it was more like the opposite. "What did you do?" she screamed right at me. Elizabeth tried to hold her back, and I was still trying to get to her, but there was no way. My cop was practically dragging me to the car.

"Let me go!" I told him. "I need to talk to her!"

"You can call your girlfriend later," he said.

"I trusted you!" Zoe yelled. "I thought you were different!"

Every word was like a punch in the stomach.

"Zoe, I didn't have a choice!" I said.

She pointed over at Mikayla, where they'd just pulled that pistol off her.

"Why would you go after her like that?" she asked.

I didn't even understand the question. Shouldn't that gun have spoken for itself?

"Is she the one who did this to you?" I asked. "She is, isn't she?"

Zoe just shook her head and didn't answer. It was like we were suddenly strangers. Or worse. More like she hated me.

"Let's go," the cop said. We were at his cruiser now, and he'd already opened the back door.

"Get in!" he told me.

I tried to pull my arm free one more time. "Hang on! Am I being detained?" I asked. "Because if not—"

He practically laughed in my face. "You watch too much TV," he said. "Just get in the car. *Right now!*"

Zoe wasn't done with me yet, either. "I brought you here to help people!" she yelled. "And now you do this?"

Elizabeth, and Mr. Knight, and a whole bunch of others were looking at me, too. And for the first time, I *did* want to get away. Because I wasn't a good

202

guy here. Not to them. Not anymore. I was a bad guy, just like the cops and all the others.

And I didn't have the first idea about how to make it right.

Like maybe ever again.

# CHAPTER 32

"ARE YOU MRS. Cross?"

"Yes. I'm this young man's great-grandmother. What's happened?"

"Ali here has gotten himself involved in a couple of matters—"

"A *couple* of matters?" Nana Mama said, and looked at me standing there on our front stoop with the cop. "What on earth happened to you? Oh, my Lord!"

She'd just seen my broken tooth, and all I wanted

to do was press pause, as much as I've ever wanted anything.

"We've already contacted Detective Cross. He's on his way," the cop told her.

"Thank you, officer," Nana said, and steered me right inside, closing the door behind us. "Does it hurt? I'm calling Dr. Villaseñor right now."

"It doesn't hurt," I told her. But I could feel that broken edge, like a little piece of glass in my mouth.

Dad showed up pretty quick, too. I wasn't sure what to expect, but he kept a lid on whatever he wanted to say until we'd been to Dr. Villaseñor's for my emergency appointment.

That was a whole thing, too. I had to get a temporary piece put on my tooth while they made a permanent one. Which meant I'd have to go back.

But that was the least of my problems. Because once we were in the car again, Dad called off the truce and really let me have it.

"You know, I was actually thinking we needed to start giving you a little more freedom," he told me. "You've been saying how your rules haven't changed since fourth grade, and that seemed like a reasonable point to me. But it's not a conversation we're going to have anymore. You really blew this, Ali. I'm just glad something worse didn't happen."

"I wasn't trying to make trouble," I said. "I was trying to help."

Dad wasn't even listening, though.

"*And* you skipped school," he said. "Is this the first time you've done that?"

"Yes, sir," I said. Still, I knew how disappointed he was.

But didn't it count for something that I was trying to help people experiencing homelessness when this happened? Or that I might have actually done something real to help solve Zoe's case?

I also wanted to tell Dad about how the police had acted, and how they'd treated me so differently when they found out I was a cop's kid. But none of it erased the fact that I'd skipped school. And Dad definitely wasn't done talking about that part.

"As of this moment, you're grounded for at least a week. We'll see," Dad said. "You're also giving up whatever you *think* this investigation of yours has been. You haven't proven yourself even remotely capable of handling something like that."

"That's not true!" I said back. "I'm good at this, Dad, and you know it."

It wasn't what I'd been waiting to say, but it just came out. I kept going, too.

"I may do stuff I shouldn't, and I know I'm going to be punished," I said. "But you know what else? When Gabe was missing, I was the first one to find out who he was with. And I might have just found out who shot Zoe, too, before the police did. You should tell them to use me more, not less."

Dad just blinked a couple of times. I don't think he could believe I was saying all that. In a way, I couldn't believe it, either.

It's not like I thought he was going to turn around and magically deputize me for giving a good speech. But you know what else? Maybe he should have.

Seriously. I know I'm *just* a kid. And I know there's all kinds of things I'm not qualified to do, or just plain shouldn't do, because of my age. But who ever said that meant a kid couldn't also be useful? Maybe even in ways that an adult never could.

I was really mad now, partly because my investigation had just crashed and burned. But also because I was tired—dead tired—of people not taking me seriously. Including Dad, sometimes.

"With everything that's happened, this is what you want to talk about?" Dad asked. "Your investigative skills?"

"I'm just trying to do whatever's best for Zoe," I said. "Hundred percent. Isn't that exactly the kind of choice you've been raising me to make? Isn't that what you do for a living? We need more *good* cops, Dad. And I think I'm going to be one someday."

Dad took a deep breath. I could tell he knew I was right about all that. *And* we both knew it wasn't just that simple.

"None of that gives you any license to leave school the way you did, much less to go to that camp, *much less* without permission," Dad said.

"But I just—"

"Do you even hear how many things are wrong with that sentence?" he said over me. I don't think I'd ever seen him so steamed before. And he's a homicide detective, so just think about that for a second.

"Can we just go home, please?" I asked. I was wiped out. My mouth was numb from the dentist, and all I wanted to do was get back to my room, close the door, and try to sort this all out.

"We're not going home," Dad said. "Detective Matheson is waiting to speak with you."

"Right now?" I asked.

"You wanted to be a part of this? Well, you got your wish. So pull it together, because we're headed to MPD," Dad said. "Welcome to the real world, son."

# ALEX CROSS

ALEX TOOK ALI to his cubicle on the third floor of the Daly Building, and parked him there. Matheson passed through the office soon after that.

"Hey, sorry, we're a little stacked right now. Ali, I'll be right with you," he said.

"He can wait," Alex answered. It was hard to know how best to wrap Ali's head around the choices he'd made that day. The most Alex could do for now was give them both some time to cool off.

He left Ali where he was and followed Matheson back up the hall. "What have you got?" he asked the younger detective. "Has she confessed to the shooting?"

If Matheson was put out by the questions, he didn't say so. But he also didn't stop walking as they talked. It was a technique Alex used himself, whenever he didn't want to be pinned down by someone at work.

"I guess you could call it a confession," Matheson said. "She's saying Zoe Knight was a 'spoiled rich girl' and that she was just trying to roll her over for some cash when the gun 'went off by accident.'" Matheson stopped at the third floor elevator bank and pushed the call button. "Yeah, and she's probably got a bridge to sell me, too," he said.

"So you don't buy it?" Alex asked.

"Not the way she's telling it, anyway," Matheson said. "I'm waiting on ballistics. We'll see if that weapon is a match, and take it from there. Meanwhile, she's squared away with Child and Family Services for the night."

"What?" Alex asked. "How old is this girl?" He'd been assuming that Mikayla Dunbar was an adult.

"Sixteen," Matheson answered. "She ran away from a group home about six months ago, and she's been living on the street since. Mostly over at that encampment where everything went south today. She'll be better off, in any case."

*Well, maybe,* Alex thought. Based on what he knew about the system in DC, not every kid in a group home was better off than every kid on the streets out there. It was heartbreaking, but true.

Still, Matheson was right about one thing. This didn't add up, especially if Zoe had known all along who the shooter was.

"Have you talked to Zoe Knight?" Alex asked.

"Of course."

"And?"

The elevator arrived. Matheson got on and turned around to face Alex.

"And I'm going to wait for ballistics, then take it from there," he said, retreating to his usual tight-lipped approach. If Ali weren't so involved in the case, Matheson probably wouldn't have even let loose as much as he had.

"I'll swing back to speak with your son in a few," Matheson said.

And before Alex could say or ask anything else, the doors slid closed.

# CHAPTER 33

I TEXTED ZOE while I was waiting to talk to Detective Matheson.

Zoe, I'm really sorry I made you so mad. I hope you can understand that I didn't have a choice. Can we talk?

Even if Zoe did hate me now, I didn't have any regrets about telling the cops about Mikayla's gun. I'd do the same thing again, and I wasn't going to apologize for that.

Still, I wanted to talk to Zoe in the worst way.

Was I right about Mikayla? Is that who she'd been covering for?

And if so, why? What did Mikayla have over her? Was it some kind of blackmail situation?

Zoe didn't answer my text, though. I tried one more time, and then I left it alone.

When Dad finally came back, he brought me over to someone's office where they could close the door and hear what I had to say. Matheson came in a minute later, and sat behind the desk across from the two of us.

"What's going on with Mikayla?" I asked right away.

"Don't concern yourself with that," Matheson said. Like I'd ever *not* concern myself with that. "I want to know what you know, Ali. Or at least, what you think you know, about Zoe Knight's shooting. And I want you to start from the beginning."

I felt like I was all in at that point. The only way to get through this now was to just keep telling the truth.

I started with what happened at Anacostia Park

that day, and what I'd seen, and how Zoe had asked me to keep it to myself, which I hadn't done. That much, Matheson had already heard from me.

Then I told him how the boots and coat (or sweater) I saw were similar to the ones Mikayla had been wearing at the K Street encampment. And I told him about spotting the gun she was carrying that morning, too.

"I think she's the one who shot Zoe," I said, "and I think Zoe's been protecting her, but I don't know why. I also don't know if it has anything to do with Dee-Cee's ex-boyfriend, Orlando, but I do know that he at least had the opportunity to be at the park that day."

From the way Matheson looked at Dad, he seemed pretty surprised about how much I had to say. I don't think Dad was surprised, though. Mostly, he still seemed mad. I just hoped he could be mad *and* a little proud of me at the same time.

"Anything else?" Matheson asked.

"Maybe," I said. "I don't know if it has anything to do with Zoe, but I do know that Darnell and Kim were arguing on Saturday night, and they said something about the police. Also, as far as I can tell, Dee-Cee wasn't part of any of this. And neither was Zoe's dad, I'd say, but I barely know him."

Matheson scribbled some more notes before he looked up again.

"Impressive," he said. "I hope you're thinking about getting into law enforcement someday."

"*Some*day," Dad said. As in, not anytime soon.

I tried getting in a few questions of my own, but Matheson wasn't talking. No surprise there. I was still going to have to wait for any word on Mikayla.

As for Zoe, I had a text waiting for me when Dad and I got back to the car. I was psyched to see her name on my phone, and even a little happy for a second there.

But then I read the text itself, and went right back to not knowing *what* to think.

ZOE KNIGHT:

You don't know me

You don't owe me

You don't ever need to care

I let you in

I didn't win

I shouldn't have brought you there
It's done, it's through
It's me, not you
It wasn't worth your time
Another day
Another play
Another wasted rhyme
Take care, Ali
ZK

# CHAPTER 34

ZOE DIDN'T COME to school the next day or Friday. That wasn't an all-bad thing for me, since I was so confused by that poem of hers. I wasn't sure if she'd broken up with me, or if we'd even been boyfriend and girlfriend to begin with, or what.

Ruby said I should just give her some space. And since I didn't have much choice, that's what I did.

In social studies, Mrs. Achebe showed us a movie. It was a documentary called *Walking While Black*, all about the issues between the African American

219

community and the police in this country. The movie was everything we'd been talking about, and it showed lots of different people with different opinions about what needed to be done.

The whole time we watched that movie, I kept coming back to one thing. Why hadn't those cops helped me at the homeless camp when I was there on the ground, bleeding and hurt? Was it just because they had Mikayla to deal with? Did they have to make a hard choice because so much was going on?

Or did they ignore me because I was just another Black kid to them? Maybe they thought I was experiencing homelessness, too. If I had to guess, I'd say that's exactly what it was about, considering how fast they changed their tune after I told them I was Alex Cross's son.

Still, the movie wasn't *all* about the bad stuff. There was also a whole section about how people and police departments can come together to talk about this kind of thing. One city had a program called Coffee with a Cop, where regular people sat down with police officers and just talked, with no agenda. And another guy had an approach that he called L-O-V-E.

L for "Learn about the community."

O for "Open your heart."

V for "Volunteer to be part of the solution."

E for "Empower others to do the same."

"That's corny," Eddie said.

"Well if *learning,* and *opening,* and *volunteering,* and *empowering* are corny, I don't know," Mrs. Achebe said. "Is that really the world you want to live in?" Her T-shirt today said, MY OTHER CAR IS A BROOM. Mrs. Achebe wasn't always super serious. But she *was* always about the love.

I raised my hand then. "I want to say something," I said. "Mostly to you, Patrice, but also to everyone."

Patrice wasn't the only person I'd been sparking with about this stuff, but it felt like she was the main one, anyway. So I told them all about how I'd seen some messed-up stuff on the street that had me thinking. I didn't say anything about Zoe, or her dad, or any of that, but I did say that I was working on my report about people experiencing homelessness when this happened, and how the police hadn't handled it very well.

"I told you so," Patrice said. "This is exactly what I've been talking about the whole time."

"I hear you," I said. "I've always heard what you were saying, even if you didn't believe me."

"Well...I'm sorry that happened to you," Patrice said, and looked at me like maybe we were seeing just a little eye-to-eye for once.

"Thanks," I said. "And you're right. It shouldn't happen to anyone."

"We also shouldn't be waiting around for the adults to do something about this stuff," Patrice added, and I agreed with that, too.

Mrs. Achebe spoke up next. "It was Henry Thoreau who said, 'Be not simply good. Be good for something.' So what do you kids want to be good *for*? What next steps would you like to take?"

"What do you think we should do?" Carmela Lipton asked.

"Nope," Mrs. Achebe said. "What do *you* think? That rally outside the school the other day was an excellent start. But what else? What's something that might have a lasting impact?"

"Something more like that movie, maybe?" Patrice asked.

"Yeah," Destiny said. "We could do some event at school, but record it and make it available for people afterward."

"I like that," I said.

"So do I," Mrs. Achebe said.

"We could use our social studies reports," Patrice said. "Call the whole thing 'My Washington,' and do like an open house, and use it to talk all about how things could be better here."

"Maybe Dee-Cee Knight could even perform," Carmela said. "Ruby Sandoval's writing about her, isn't she?"

"I think so," I said. I didn't know what was true anymore. "I'll ask Ruby."

"Can't you just ask Zoe about it?" Patrice asked. "I mean, you guys are like a thing now, right?"

I wasn't sure what to say to that.

"I'll look into it," was all I told them, only 'cause

I didn't have the nerve to say that getting Zoe involved in anything I was working on right now had somewhere between a zero chance of happening…and a zero chance of happening.

But it was a start, anyway. Maybe if we saw this through, at least something good could come out of it.

# ALEX CROSS

**ALEX WASN'T HOLDING** his breath waiting around for Detective Matheson to report back on the Zoe Knight case. He spent the day periodically checking the departmental files to see if there was any news.

Then, just before five o'clock, an update was posted.

Apparently, the gun that had been found on Mikayla Dunbar was a forensic match for the bullet that had broken Zoe Knight's wrist. That was no surprise, given Mikayla's story, even if her confession had been a bit sketchy.

Also, the report said, in addition to finding Mikayla's fingerprints on the weapon, the MPD lab had turned up a few older, trace prints belonging to Orlando Fletcher.

Alex read the last few lines of the report a second time. Somehow, it seemed, Mikayla had come into possession of Orlando's gun. Whether that happened before or after Zoe was shot, the report didn't say. Still, this was major.

Alex didn't even bother texting Matheson or dialing his number for more information. The shift supervisor, Sergeant Rook, would almost certainly be as up-to-date as anyone on this. And unlike Detective Matheson, Rook had always been a team player, ready to share information where it was needed.

"George, it's Alex Cross," he said, when Rook picked up. "I'm seeing some new activity in the Zoe Knight file?"

"Yeah," he said. "It's turning out not to be so straightforward."

"So I see," Alex told him. "Can you tell me any more at this point?"

"Matheson and a couple of patrol officers are on their way over to Orlando Fletcher's apartment right now," Rook told him. "That's all I have, but we should know more soon."

Alex hung up, thinking mostly about Ali. Despite how rough the last day or so had been, he couldn't help feeling a little sorry for his son. Ali had really poured himself into this case, and it couldn't be easy sitting home, just waiting and wondering about what might happen next.

*Oh, well,* Alex thought. It couldn't be helped. He'd bring Ali up to speed just as soon as it made sense to do so. In the meantime, the boy would just have to be patient.

# CHAPTER 35

I WAS STUCK at home after school that day, with no phone or computer privileges. Dad said I was grounded for a week, which stunk. But I got my homework done in record time, anyway, including some more research for my report. I'd already decided to stick with the same topic, even if Zoe never spoke to me again.

But I was also going crazy, wondering what was up with everyone.

Then, just after five o'clock, the doorbell rang.

I stayed in my room, listening while Nana Mama answered the door.

"Hi, Mrs. Cross," I heard Ruby saying. "Can we please talk to Ali?"

"I'm sorry, children, but Ali isn't allowed to have friends over," Nana said.

"We know," Gabe said next. "But it's *really* important. Please? Just for a minute?"

By now I was out in the hall, still listening, but I didn't go any closer. Something told me if Nana Mama saw me, she'd remember to be strict.

It was a good bet, too.

"All right," Nana said. "Five minutes, in the living room. I don't want any secret conversations going on."

"No problem, ma'am," Ruby said. "Thank you."

"Ali!" Nana called up, but I was already on my way down the stairs.

When I saw Ruby and Gabe, both of them were looking at me with eyes big as dinner plates. Something was definitely going on.

We all sat down in the living room, including Nana Mama.

"What have you got?" I asked.

*"This,"* Gabe said. He flipped open his laptop and started pulling something up, while Ruby did the same thing on her phone.

"So, here's Orlando Fletcher," Gabe said. He'd loaded some Instagram account, and clicked one of the posts to make it bigger. It showed a tall, thin Black guy, holding a rack of glasses, working at some bar. The caption just said, "Our intrepid dishwasher, Orlando Fletcher."

"This is from a bar called Cavalcade," Gabe said. "It's only a few blocks from Orlando's apartment."

"Okay?" I said.

"So he's working two jobs," Gabe said. "At the garage, and at the bar."

"Okay?" I said again.

Ruby held out her phone for me to see next. "And here's Kim's Insta from last Saturday night," she said.

The picture was a selfie Kim had taken, along with two other women. All three of them were holding up fancy-looking drinks. And the caption said,

"Call me Ms. Blige cuz I am all about #NoMore-Drama tonight. Happy weekend, y'all!"

"Just guess where that is?" Ruby said.

It was coming together now. "Cavalcade?" I said.

*"Cavalcade,"* Ruby said.

*"Boo-yah!"* Gabe said. We all stopped and looked over at him. I guess he was just trying that one on, but he shrugged now. "Or...not."

"Anyway, yeah," Ruby went on. "Kim left the party at Dee-Cee's at like eight-thirty on Saturday night, and this was posted just before eleven."

"And Orlando doesn't work weekends at the garage," I said.

"Cause he probably works Saturday nights at this place," Gabe said.

"Exactly."

It felt like an actual *click*! Like something had just fallen into place.

"So, do you think Orlando and Kim are—"

"A couple? Yeah," Ruby said.

So Dee-Cee's ex-boyfriend, the guy she'd kicked out of her house, was now seeing her sister on the side. And it looked like they were keeping it a secret, too.

"What do you think it means?" Gabe asked.

For one thing, I thought, it meant that I'd gotten it wrong with Dad the day before. I'd told him all about how good I was at this stuff. But the truth was, *we* were good at it. Not just me.

And there was more.

"Cedric and Mateo are over at Orlando's apartment building right now, just scoping it out for us," Ruby said. "Let me try them."

She put in a FaceTime call then, and Cedric showed up on the screen a second later.

"Hey," he said.

"How's it going over there?" Ruby asked.

"Boring," Mateo said from off-camera.

"We're also out of snacks," Cedric said.

"Very funny," Ruby said.

"We don't even know if Orlando's home," Mateo said. "Seriously, you guys, this feels like a waste of time."

"Thanks for going anyway," I said. "No sign of Kim?"

"Nope," Cedric said. "But it's early, right? Maybe she'll—"

Cedric had just trailed off. His screen went blurry, and it seemed like he was on the move all of a sudden.

"Cedric?" Ruby said. "What's up?"

"Oh...wow," Cedric said. *"No way."*

Ruby, Gabe, and I were looking at one another. Even Nana had come around the back of the couch to see.

"What's going on?" I asked.

Cedric's face came back on the screen then. "You guys, you guys, you're not going to believe this," he said, whispering now. "Check it out."

The phone in his hand spun around one-eighty in another blur, and then stopped. That's when I saw Detective Matheson and a police officer getting out of a patrol car and heading over to the front door of Orlando's building to ring the bell.

# CHAPTER 36

WE WATCHED LONG enough to see them bring Orlando outside. Cedric hung back with his phone pointed that way, but none of us said anything the whole time. Orlando wasn't cuffed, and he wasn't resisting, either. He just let them put him in the back of a car and they drove away.

Whatever all that meant.

"Someone needs to tell my dad about this," I said. "Because it can't be me."

"You don't think he already knows?" Cedric asked.

"I doubt it," I said. "I think Detective Matheson is keeping most of this stuff to himself."

"*I'll* tell him," Nana said. "Meanwhile..." She leaned across the couch to look into Ruby's phone again. "Cedric, go home! Mateo, does your father even know where you are?"

"Not exactly," Mateo said. "But I'm only a couple of blocks from my house."

"Well, good," Nana said. "Because I'm giving you fifteen minutes to text me a picture of yourself at your front door, nice and clear. If I don't hear from you by then, I *will* be calling your parents. You, too, Cedric. Understood?"

"Um..." was all Cedric got to say.

"I'll have Ruby text you my number," Nana said.

It's like she has a foolproof system for everything. About a second later, Cedric and Mateo were on their way home. And a second after *that,* Nana started shooing Ruby and Gabe out the front door.

"All right, you two. I hope you have a wonderful evening, but you can't stay here," she told them.

I was surprised she'd let everything go that far, so I wasn't going to complain about cutting it short. But I did still need to talk to Ruby. In about half a minute, she and Gabe were going to be up the street and gone, and I'd be stuck at home with no computer or phone privileges. If I didn't catch her now, I'd have to wait until Monday morning at school.

So as soon as Nana headed for the kitchen, I went to the front door, opened it, and yelled outside. "Hey, Ruby, you forgot your phone!" Then I closed the door behind me and caught up with them on the sidewalk outside.

"I didn't forget my phone," Ruby said.

"I know," I said, and pretended to hand her something, just in case Nana was watching. "I wanted to ask what was up with Zoe. Have you talked to her? I mean…about me?"

Ruby looked at the ground, like there was something interesting down there. "I don't know, Ali," she said.

"You don't know if you talked to her?" I asked.

"Um, no." Ruby said. "I mean, I can't just tell you what she said. That's up to Zoe."

So at least I knew they *had* been talking about me.

"Far as I can tell, she broke up with me in a text," I said. "Unless she was never my girlfriend to begin with. I don't know *what's* going on. Help me out?"

Ruby gave me another look, like I was making this hard for her. And maybe I was, but I didn't care. I just wanted to find out what was up with Zoe.

"It wasn't *just* a text," Ruby said. "She sent you a freaking poem, okay? You don't do that if you don't still care. That's all I'm going to say."

It was something, anyway. I think it even counted as good news. So I didn't push it any further.

"What about the investigation?" I asked. "Do you know if Mikayla confessed to the shooting?"

Ruby shook her head. "I don't know," she said. "For real. Zoe didn't say anything about that either way."

I wondered why not. Did that mean Zoe was in the dark about Mikayla? Or was she just keeping it to herself?

"Can you try to find out?" I asked.

Just then, I heard the front door open, and Nana called down.

"Ali! Are you *trying* to exhaust my patience?" When I looked up, she was waving at me to get back in the house. "Come on. Let's go!"

I shrugged at Gabe and Ruby. "Guess I'll see you guys Monday," I said.

"Later," Gabe said, and turned to get out of there. I think he was more scared of Nana than any of my other friends. Then again, Gabe was also smarter than any of my other friends, so you do the math.

"See you Monday," Ruby said. "And . . . I'll try."

She couldn't say too much with Nana right there, but she meant she'd try to get some info from Zoe. In the meantime, all I could do was wait. And anyone who knows me knows that waiting isn't exactly my best subject in life.

It was going to be a long weekend.

# CHAPTER 37

I WASN'T EXPECTING to hear from Ruby until we were back at school. So when Nana's phone rang in the middle of breakfast the next morning, and Ruby's name showed up on her screen, I knew something big was up.

"What in the world?" Nana said. "Hello? Ruby?"

There was a long silence while she listened to whatever Ruby was telling her.

"Slow down, sweetheart. Let me put you on with Ali's dad," Nana said, and handed the phone over while Bree, Jannie, and I just sat there letting our cereal get soggy.

Right away, I could see on Dad's face that something was wrong. He kept looking over at me, too. I didn't know for sure if it was about Zoe, but what else could it be?

"I'll ask him," Dad said finally. "Just sit tight. We'll let you know as soon as we learn anything."

"What's going on?" I asked once he'd hung up.

"Have you been in touch with Zoe since yesterday?" Dad asked. "I need you to be honest, Ali."

"No," I said. "I swear. I haven't talked to her since the tent camp. Why? What's going on?"

"Ruby got a call from Zoe's aunt Kim this morning," Dad said. "Apparently, Zoe didn't sleep at home last night."

"Where's Dee-Cee?" Bree asked.

"Out of town for a couple of shows, apparently," Dad answered.

"Wait, so Zoe's *missing*?" I asked.

"It's too soon to say for sure," Dad said.

That wasn't very reassuring. With everything going on, I could imagine all kinds of reasons why

Zoe might want to disappear. I could imagine a few reasons why someone *else* might want her to disappear, too, which was even scarier.

"What about Zoe's father?" I asked.

"Ruby didn't say anything about him," Dad told me.

"Ruby doesn't *know* about him," I said. "I guess it's a secret that he's experiencing homelessness. But he and Zoe are pretty tight. We could go over to that camp on K Street and see if he's around."

Dad gave me a long hard look. I think he trusted my instincts, but we both knew those same instincts had gotten me into a lot of trouble the last few days.

Still, I think Dad knew I could help. For starters, I was the only one who knew what Zoe's father looked like.

"We just need half an hour," I said. "If he's not there, we can come right back."

"All right," Dad said. "But you're still grounded. As long as we're out of the house, *I'm* your home base. Got it?"

I started putting on my shoes by the back door

right away. "What about Detective Matheson?" I asked. "Do you need to call him?"

Dad thought about it for a second. "I'll call him when we find Zoe," he said.

"Sounds good to me," I said.

I liked how he said *when* we find Zoe, not *if* we find Zoe. And even more than that, I liked how he said *we* were going to be the ones to do it.

Because obviously, I was all in.

# CHAPTER 38

DAD DROVE US straight over to K Street. When we got there, it looked like a lot of people hadn't come back after that sweep the other day.

Last time, I'd seen about twenty tents on either side of the street. Now, there were maybe six, all clustered on one side.

Still, I was feeling some nerves. If anyone from the other day recognized me, this could get ugly all over again. The only thing anyone knew about me here was that I had snitched on Mikayla. So I was glad Dad came along this time.

"Can we just walk down and back?" I asked. I remembered that Zoe's dad had a light-green tent, and I didn't see it in that cluster. But I wanted to make sure.

Before we got very far, I saw Elizabeth getting out of her tent and standing up to stretch.

"Dad! I know her!" I said, and picked up my pace. He put a hand on my shoulder, though, and slowed me down enough to stick by him as we walked over together.

"Excuse me, Elizabeth?" I asked.

It took a second for her to recognize me. When she did, you could see it on her face, like I was nothing more than a bad smell.

"Is there something I can do for you?" she asked. Her voice was icy cold. It made me want to turn around and walk away, but I couldn't do that. I had to suck it up.

"This is my dad," I said. "We're trying to find Zoe."

"That right?" Elizabeth asked. She wasn't even looking at us now.

"Zoe never came home last night," Dad said. "It's not clear if she's missing, or just unaccounted for. But we were wondering if you might have seen her."

"You're police, right?" Elizabeth asked Dad. You could tell she didn't mean it in a good way. I guess Zoe had told her who my dad was after what happened with Mikayla.

"I'm off duty, but yes, ma'am," Dad answered. "We wouldn't be here asking if it wasn't important. Please, if there's anything you can tell us—"

"She and her daddy left this morning, okay?" Elizabeth said, like she wanted to get it over with. "He might gotta work today, I'm not sure."

"That's right!" I said, remembering all at once. "Zoe told me her dad works at one of the soup kitchens in the city." It was like another puzzle piece dropping into place.

But I couldn't remember which soup kitchen she'd said it was.

"Do you know where we might look?" Dad asked Elizabeth.

Now she seemed even more sketched out than before. Other people in the camp were starting to notice us, and something told me it would be bad for Elizabeth if they saw her helping the cops. Even if the "cops" right now were just Dad and me.

"You know what?" I said. "Never mind. I'll bet we can figure it out for ourselves."

I didn't have to say it twice, either.

"Mm-hm," Elizabeth said. Then she turned and went back into her tent without a good-bye or anything.

I wanted to do something for her, but even giving her some money right now seemed like the wrong thing. Like maybe it would be insulting, or look bad in front of the others.

Or maybe she would have been happy to take some cash off us. I really didn't know. But now it seemed like the best thing was to just head out and leave her alone.

I waited until we were back in the car, and then asked Dad what he thought about how I handled it.

"I'd say it was a good call," Dad said. "We know Zoe was here, and we know where to look next. That's enough."

I knew Dad didn't want to get me all geared up

246

on this investigation again, but it did feel a little like we were partners out in the field now. And I'm not going to lie. It was an awesome feeling. I *liked* working with Dad, especially after our big fight the other day.

"So, if I can get online, I could google soup kitchens around the city," I said. "Maybe we can find the place where Mr. Knight works."

"Worth a try," Dad said.

"There's just one problem," I told him. "See, I'm kind of grounded, and my father took away my phone privileges."

*"He did?"* Dad asked, playing along while he handed over his phone and pulled away from the curb. "That guy sounds like a jerk."

I smiled now, too.

"Nah," I said. "He's okay."

# CHAPTER 39

**WE STRUCK OUT** at the first three soup kitchens we visited. By the time we got to District Community Kitchen, it was hopping. People were lined up for lunch, out the door and around the corner. I noticed there were all kinds of folks getting something to eat, including kids my age. And not everybody looked poor, either. A few people were in suits and ties.

I stuck it all away like mental notes for my social

studies report, even if that wasn't job number one right now.

Inside, the cafeteria was jammed, but we spotted Zoe's father right away. You could see straight into the kitchen, where Mr. Knight was stirring a huge pot of something on the stove.

"Can I help you?" a lady in the serving line asked. "If you want to eat, you're going to have to get to the back of the line."

"I'm Detective Cross from MPD," Dad said. This time, he showed his badge. "I was hoping to have a quick word with Mr. Knight over there."

The lady looked carefully at Dad's ID, and then over her shoulder at Zoe's father. She seemed like she wasn't sure what to do.

"It's about his daughter," Dad said. "She might be missing."

"Oh, it's about *Zoe*?" the lady said.

"That's right," Dad told her.

"Hey, Stephen!" the lady yelled into the kitchen, and he looked up. "This officer here is looking for *Zoe*! Can you come out here and talk to him?"

I didn't know why she was shouting, but there was definitely something weird about the whole thing. Mr. Knight held up a finger to say *just a second* and went to turn down the stove.

"You two can meet in the office, if you like," the lady told Dad, and pointed to a door on the opposite side of the room. She caught Mr. Knight's eye and pointed him that way, too.

"Wait here," Dad told me.

I was already looking around and taking the whole place in, trying to figure out what the weird vibe was about. And when I'd turned one-eighty to look back the way we'd come in, I saw someone leaving the cafeteria in a hurry.

Not just someone. *Zoe.*

Probably, anyway.

Almost definitely.

I'd barely caught sight of whoever it was. But the one thing I'd seen for sure was a flash of red in the person's right hand, just before they ducked into the hall. It was the same color red as that poetry notebook Zoe always carried around.

Also, I'd just figured out why the cafeteria lady

was saying Zoe's name so loud. She was trying to warn her, in case Zoe didn't want to be found. That was my theory, anyway. And there was only one way to prove it.

I looked back at the office where I could see Dad and Mr. Knight just sitting down to talk. If I went all the way over there and told Dad what was up, I'd lose Zoe for sure. Was that a risk I was willing to take?

*No,* I thought. *Definitely not.*

And about half a second later, I was heading for the door.

# CHAPTER 40

IT WAS QUIET in the hall, like a school on summer break. I didn't even know whether to go left or right—until I heard a slam, somewhere off to my right.

I fast-walked that direction, and around a corner where the hall ended at another door. When I opened it, I found a staircase leading up. I could hear someone running on the steps, but I still couldn't see who it was.

So I stayed quiet and kept going.

The stairs went back and forth, half a floor for

every switchback. I was just past the second floor when I heard another door slam, somewhere higher up. I started going two steps at a time and passed an exit for the third floor, which was locked, then the fourth floor, also locked, before the stairs dead-ended at the top, with one more door.

This had to be the roof access, I figured. An old cardboard box was sitting on the landing, and I used it to prop open the door as I let myself outside.

It was super-hot up there. The sun was pounding down, and my eyes took a second to adjust. Not that there was much to see. Just an empty roof, a water tower, and a big air-conditioning compressor. When I listened, all I heard was the sound of traffic down below.

I moved slowly, walking a half circle around the little shed structure that housed the door I'd come through. That gave me a sight line to the corners of the roof I hadn't been able to see yet.

And there she was. When I spotted Zoe, she was already on the roof of the next building over. An aluminum extension ladder was set up like a bridge between the two, and she'd obviously just crossed it. Beyond that, I could see a familiar green tent and a couple of lawn chairs, like a little rooftop camp next door.

"Zoe!" I yelled.

When she stopped and turned around, she was squinting into the sun. "Ali?" she yelled back. "What do you want?"

"What does it look like?" I said. "I want to talk to you. Hold up!"

I climbed onto that makeshift bridge and tried not to look down. It was a five-story drop into the alley below me, and my insides flipped just thinking about it.

Oh, man! Dad was going to kill me...if I didn't do it to myself first.

I went hand by hand, step by step, keeping a grip on the sides of the ladder, and using the rungs to push off with my feet in a low bear crawl. At least Zoe wasn't running away from me anymore.

"You don't give up, do you?" she asked.

"Not until you tell me why you're hiding like this," I said, and jumped down onto the roof next to her. "What's going on? Are you okay?"

Zoe gave me a long look. Then she took a deep breath and sat down right there, with her knees pulled up. I sat next to her and tilted my head, trying to see her face. Her braids got in the way, but I could see tears dripping onto the ground between her feet.

I'd never seen Zoe cry before. Not even after she got shot in the wrist.

"This is all my fault," she said. "I never should have...I mean...I never thought..."

She couldn't even finish what she was saying. It made me want to cry, too, but I held it in and put an arm around her shoulder.

"Zoe?" I said. "Whatever's going on, I've got your back. Just let me help you, if I can."

"I know I'm in all kinds of trouble," she said. "I just couldn't deal. I had to get away."

"Does your mom know where you are?" I asked.

She nodded and wiped her eyes on her sleeve. "Momma's coming home this afternoon," she said. "I'll see her later."

"I think your Aunt Kim is really worried about you, too," I said.

"Yeah, like Kim cares about anything but herself," Zoe said, sounding more mad than sad now. I was pretty sure I knew what that meant, too.

"So, you know about her and Orlando?" I asked.

Zoe looked up, and her eyes got big. "How do *you* know about her and Orlando?"

"I've been watching," I said. "We all have—me, Ruby, Gabe, Cedric, and Mateo. But only because we care."

She still looked confused, but she didn't push it. "Anyway," she said. "That's really what all of this has been about."

"All of *what*, though?" I asked. "Can you please just start at the beginning?"

Part of me was thinking I should let Dad know where we were. But the other part of me was more like, *just wait*. It seemed like I was about to get the whole story here, and I didn't want to interrupt. Dad always says the key to interviewing witnesses is more about listening than asking questions.

So I waited.

And then, finally, Zoe started talking.

# CHAPTER 41

"So, REMEMBER WHEN I went to look for Momma backstage at the festival that day?" Zoe asked. "Right before this all went down?"

"Yeah?" I said. How could I forget? That was the last time I saw her before she got shot.

"I was actually going back there to meet Mikayla," she said. "The whole thing was supposed to be super simple. I paid her a hundred dollars, and she was going to fire into the side of Momma's trailer with one of Orlando's guns, to make it look like he'd done it."

It was a whole lot of new information all at once, and took me a second just to figure out what she was saying. Even then, all I could think to ask was one little question.

"Why?" I said.

"Because Orlando's a piece of garbage," Zoe said. "When he lived with us, he was always taking money with Momma's ATM card and coming home drunk. He'd get up in Momma's face, making threats, throwing stuff. I made her call the cops a couple of times, but they never did a thing."

I already knew Zoe hated the police for the way they treated people experiencing homelessness, like her dad, like her dad, but I guess that wasn't her only reason. She said they treated her mom like some kind of nuisance when they came to the house— and one time they didn't even show up at all.

"Then one night, when she wasn't there, Orlando got mad about something, I don't even remember what. He took a pistol out of the safe and started waving it around, pointing it at me and talking trash. That's when I knew I had to make my own move."

"So you took one of Orlando's guns?" I asked.

Zoe shivered, like shaking off a bad memory. "I put it in a Ziploc bag to keep his fingerprints on there, just in case. But then he accused me of taking it, and that was the last straw for Momma. Momma kicked him out the same day, and I buried that thing in the backyard. I told myself I'd give it a year, and if Orlando stayed gone, I was just going to throw it in the river."

"And what happened?" I asked.

"What happened was, Orlando started taking up with Kim," she said. "It was supposed to be some kind of secret, but every time Momma went out of town, he came sneaking around like Mister Obvious."

"And he knew that you found out?" I asked.

"That's when he started saying bad things were going to happen to me and Momma if I told anyone. And the thing was, I believed him," she said. "I mean, why wouldn't I?"

I could see Zoe was trying not to cry again. It made me hate Orlando even more, and I'd never even met this dude. But nobody deserved to be in Zoe's shoes that way.

"I even recorded him once, just in case," Zoe said. "But the police don't do nothing until someone gets hurt for real, and then it's too late. No offense."

"It's okay, I understand," I said. "Go on."

"So, I asked Mikayla to meet me at the park that day," Zoe said. "I told her to bring gloves, to keep her prints from getting on anything. But she brought these stupid leather ones that were too big. It made everything hard to handle. She didn't even get that gun out of the Ziploc before it...you know."

"Went off accidentally?" I asked.

"Yeah," Zoe said. "I'd been telling her the whole time to give me a minute, so I could get over to the stage where Momma was, and have an alibi for later. But she didn't listen."

I thought about what Zoe's wrist looked like when we found her that day. Just remembering it felt like an invisible punch in the gut.

"So that *was* Mikayla by your mom's trailer," I said. "That's who I saw."

"For a second, anyway," Zoe answered. "She was

supposed to drop Orlando's piece and run, but I guess she kept it."

"Why didn't you turn her in?" I asked.

Zoe looked down at her cast. It was dirty now, like the color of old gum.

"I was the one who pulled her into this in the first place," she said. "It was more like we were protecting each other. Besides, what was I going to do? Turn in a girl experiencing homelessness?"

"That's why you were so mad when I got her arrested," I said, figuring it out. "I'm really sorry about that—"

"It's okay," Zoe said. "You didn't know. And I'm sorry I went off on you the way I did."

It was finally making sense. All the different pieces I'd been thinking about were fitting together now, but in a way that I never saw coming.

"How did you know Orlando would be at the park that day?" I asked.

"I sent him a text from Kim's phone that morning so he'd think it was coming from her," Zoe said. "I told him not to text back, and to meet at Momma's trailer during the show."

I was just looking at Zoe now, shaking my head. I'd always thought she was amazing, but I could see now that I'd been underestimating her this whole time.

"What?" Zoe said.

"You're like some kind of genius," I said.

"Yeah, right," she said. "And I'm going to *genius* myself all the way to juvie."

That part was starting to sink in now, too. Zoe was going to be in a lot of trouble for this. Legally speaking, it seemed mad complicated to me, but what did I know?

Before I could say anything else, Zoe's phone rang. When she took it out, I saw Dad's number on the screen.

"That's my father," I said, and she answered on speaker.

"Hey, Dad," I said. "I'm here with Zoe."

"Is she okay?" Dad asked.

"I'm okay," Zoe answered. "Thanks, Detective Cross."

"Zoe, your mom is on her way here," Dad said. "Where are you two?"

"Upstairs," I told him. "We'll be right down."

I didn't see any point in letting Dad know that "upstairs" actually meant "on the roof of the building next door." I was in enough trouble already. If he saw where I'd gotten to by now, I was going to be lucky to get un-grounded any time before the end of middle school.

The important thing was, Zoe was okay. With any luck, I could help her get through whatever came next. I just didn't know what that was going to be.

But I guess we were going to find out together.

# CHAPTER 42

I LET ZOE go back across that ladder bridge ahead of me. She didn't have two good hands to work with, so she just walked a little bent over, keeping her center of gravity low.

I stuck to my bear crawl, with my hands and feet both on the ladder. It was kind of embarrassing to crawl where Zoe had walked, but now that I wasn't 100 percent focused on finding her, it was even scarier to use that rickety makeshift bridge.

"You've got this!" Zoe said, once I was almost there.

That's when I made the mistake of looking up from what I was doing. I caught Zoe's eye for maybe half a second, but it was enough for me to lose my footing. My shoe caught on one of the ladder rungs, and I tripped, and fell forward.

The whole ladder shook. One arm and both feet fell between the rungs. For a second, I was mostly dangling over that five-story drop, waiting for the whole thing to shake right off the side of the building behind me.

"Ali!" Zoe yelled.

"I'm okay!" I said. I'd gone down hard, and my shoulder hurt, but at least I was still there. When I looked back, I saw the ladder was barely hanging on to the edge of the roof behind me. Which left zero room for error now.

My blood was pumping. I could feel it in my ears, along with a kind of rushing sound. Which I guess was the panic.

"Go slow," Zoe said.

I took it one thing at a time, and got a solid grip with my right hand, then my left, before I put my feet back on the rungs, and started moving again.

*Don't fall, don't fall, don't fall* kept going through my head, until I was close enough to put my hand in Zoe's, and she started to help pull me in.

"Almost there," she said.

I reached, and put my other hand on the ledge. And then—

There was no warning.

When the ladder came off the roof behind me, it was like a hole opening up. Suddenly, my feet didn't have anything under them but air.

"Ali!" Zoe screamed. I slammed against the side of the building, still gripping the ledge with one hand and Zoe with the other. My feet were swinging free, kicking at the wall, but it wasn't getting me anywhere.

Zoe locked her hand around my wrist, just as I heard that ladder crashing into the alley down below. It sounded like an explosion. Or a preview of what was going to happen to *me* if I didn't hold on.

"Climb!" Zoe yelled.

"I'm trying!" I said. My swinging legs just made it harder, and my weight pulled Zoe off balance. She fell forward and almost came over the edge herself.

I was screaming now—no words, just a brain full of blind fear—trying to find the strength to get where I needed to go. My whole world was a blur.

Finally, my J's caught some traction on the side of the building. I inched myself up a little higher. Zoe managed to back up a step, too.

Another rush of adrenaline pumped through me, and I pushed with my feet one more time. It was just enough to let Zoe yank me the rest of the way up, until I flopped out onto the roof, catching my breath like I'd sprinted a mile.

"Are you all right?" Zoe asked.

"I am now," I said. "I would have been roadkill if it weren't for you."

"You never would have been up here if it weren't for me," Zoe said.

We got up and looked back over the edge. Nobody was in the alley, thank God, but that ladder was

267

in about eighteen pieces of twisted metal. At least I wasn't down there with it.

And even though I never asked Zoe to keep this part to herself, I knew she would. She's pretty good at keeping secrets, after all.

Now we had one more to share.

# Chapter 43

I DIDN'T EAT breakfast on the day of Zoe's trial. Things had gotten a chance to settle down over the last week, but I couldn't say the same for my stomach that morning. I figured it was better to go hungry than it would be to boot up a belly full of bacon, eggs, and toast in the middle of my first-ever court appearance.

Zoe had already admitted to everything she'd done. That part wasn't in question, and I wasn't going to be testifying about the facts of the case.

I was going in as a character witness, I guess you'd call it.

That meant no objections, no cross-examinations, or anything like that from the lawyers. It was just going to be a conversation between me and the judge.

Still, I was feeling the pressure for sure, like an elephant on my chest. If this didn't go well, Zoe could be sent to juvenile detention for the conspiracy charge against her. That's what they called what she did, hiring Mikayla to fire off that gun in a public place.

Speaking of Mikayla, she'd already gotten sentenced to live in a halfway house until she was eighteen. Which wasn't great for her, but could have been worse. It helped that Zoe had talked her mom into hiring a lawyer for Mikayla, instead of the court-appointed one. I think Dee-Cee and Zoe were planning on looking out for her as much as they could.

Now, today, it was going to be up to the judge how seriously he wanted to take the charges against Zoe.

Dad and Bree both came with me to the Juvenile

Court Building on H Street. When we got there, the courtroom was practically empty. Zoe and her mom were sitting at one of the two tables in front, along with some guy I didn't recognize, probably their lawyer. The prosecutor assigned to Zoe's case was sitting alone at the opposite table.

I barely got a chance to sit down before they called me up to the witness stand. This was the second of two days for the trial, and I was the last witness. My guess was everyone wanted to get this over with.

"Please raise your right hand," the bailiff said. "Do you swear to tell the truth, the whole truth, and nothing but the truth, so help you God?"

"I do," I said.

It was like something straight out of a movie. I took a breath and tried to focus. My phantom breakfast—the one I never ate—felt like it wanted to come up.

Sure, no pressure.

"You may be seated," the judge told me.

A court reporter was sitting in front of the bench, tapping away on that machine of hers. The only other person around was Darnell. He sat next to Dad and Bree, in the chairs right behind the defendant's table.

Bree shot me a little thumbs-up from her seat. *You'll be fine,* she mouthed, just before Judge Shapiro started talking.

"So, Ali," he said. "Thank you for being here this morning. Is this your first time in court?"

"As a witness, yes, sir," I said. "I mean, your honor."

"Okay, then," he said. "And what is it you'd like to tell me about your friend Zoe?"

At least I knew how to start. Dad had been coaching me for this part.

"I guess I want to tell you why you should be as lenient as possible with her," I said. I looked over and Zoe smiled, but just with her mouth. Her eyes looked sad and scared at the same time.

"I've known Zoe for a while," I went on. "And I can tell you for a fact that she's a really good person—"

Judge Shapiro held up a finger to stop me.

"Good people do bad things all the time," he

said. "The question is, *why* should I be lenient? What compelling testimony can you offer this court, young man?"

He was actually trying to help. I knew that. Dad had told me about how the judge would *want* good answers. But that didn't mean he was going to make it easy for me.

"It seems like it should count for something that Zoe and her mom called the police about this more than once," I said. "They did what they were supposed to, and that didn't help. It only got worse after that."

"Are you saying that's an acceptable excuse for stealing a firearm and paying someone to discharge it in a public area?" Judge Shapiro asked me.

"No, sir," I said. I was kind of embarrassed, if that's what he thought I was saying. But I was also having a hard time making everything come out the right way. "I just mean, the people who were supposed to be protecting Zoe and her mom weren't doing their jobs."

"And what people were those?" the judge asked.

I took a deep breath.

"The police, your honor," I said. It felt weird coming out of my mouth, and I looked right out at Dad. He just nodded back, like he was telling me I was fine. So I kept going.

"I'm not trying to put anyone else down," I said. "I'm just trying to say that if someone like Zoe doesn't deserve leniency, then I don't know who does. She didn't even turn in the girl who pulled that trigger on her, because she felt responsible for what happened."

The judge squinted, like he wasn't sure what to make of that.

"So then..." The judge sat back. "Shouldn't I treat Miss Knight as the *more* responsible party? And not less?"

Oh, man. What had I just done? It was like a trap that I'd set for myself, and walked right into. I was supposed to be *helping* Zoe's case, but it felt more like I was doing the opposite.

Dad and Bree were watching, and I knew they were pulling for me, but there wasn't anything they could do to help right now. This was all on me.

"Could I start over?" I asked. "Maybe answer that

one again? I didn't really mean it the way it came out—"

"You know what? You're fine, son," Judge Shapiro said. "You can take a seat. I think I have everything I need."

"But, Your Honor—" was all I got out.

"We'll take a short recess and I'll be back with my decision," the judge said. Just like that, everyone was standing up and Shapiro was on his way out of the courtroom.

Now I was straight-up panicking. My face was hot, and my breathing was getting faster as I walked back to my seat.

I looked over at Zoe one more time. She had her eyes down, and wouldn't look over, like she knew the same thing I did. I'd just blown the one chance I was going to have for helping her out.

I'd wanted to step up when it mattered most. Instead, I choked. And if something bad happened to Zoe because of this, I was never going to forgive myself.

# CHAPTER 44

AS SOON AS I got out to the hall, I looked around for a bathroom sign. When I spotted it, I sprinted straight for that door.

I got as far as the sink before I puked up whatever was in my stomach, which wasn't much. My eyes were watering, but I was crying, too. What had I done? How could I have just made things even worse for Zoe?

"Hey, bud," I heard Dad's voice behind me.

"I messed up, bad," I told Dad. "After everything

Zoe's been through, she's going to get sent away because of me."

"You don't know that," Dad said. "I've learned the hard way that it doesn't help to make predictions at this point. Let's wait and see what Judge Shapiro has to say."

I knew that Dad was super smart about this stuff, but none of it made my heart hurt any less. I couldn't even go back into the hall and face Zoe right now.

"Can I just stay here for a minute?" I asked.

"Of course." Dad rubbed my back and handed me a bottle of water. For a long time, neither of us said anything.

Then, finally, he spoke up again.

"Listen, you've had a rough couple of weeks, to say the least," he told me. "And when this is behind us, I think you should talk to a counselor."

"Like a shrink?" I asked. "What for?"

"I didn't push it after the shooting at the park," Dad said. "But between what happened to Zoe, and your time at that tent camp, and all the pressure at school, as a cop's kid? It adds up."

"I know," I said. "But I'm handling it."

"You are," Dad said. "Like a champ. I mean that. I couldn't be prouder to call you my son right now. But 'handling it' doesn't always mean figuring it out on your own. Sometimes, it's about getting a little help."

"Do I have to?" I asked.

"No," Dad said right away. That surprised me. "What I want is for you to go because you trust me. My gut says you could use someone to talk to. Someone who doesn't know you, and doesn't have any skin in the game."

I thought about it. The fact was, I trusted Dad more than anyone else in the world. He made me mad sometimes, but that was a separate issue.

"Okay," I said. "I'll try it."

"Great," Dad said. "I'll set up three appointments with a therapist I know, and we can take stock after that, see how it's going."

There was a knock on the bathroom door then, and Darnell came in.

"Hey, guys," he said. "Shapiro's coming back with a ruling."

278

"All right," Dad said, and put his hands on my shoulders. "You ready?"

I looked at Dad, and a whole new wave of nervous washed over me. "I don't know about *ready*," I said. "But let's do this."

A minute later, everyone was back where they'd started and Judge Shapiro was sitting up at the bench again.

"Young lady, would you please rise?" Shapiro asked.

Zoe, Dee-Cee, and their lawyer all got out of their chairs at the same time.

Here it went.

"Miss Knight, this court takes the charges against you quite seriously," Judge Shapiro said. My stomach got a little tighter, like someone was tying knots down there. "I also recognize that there are extenuating circumstances in this case, and that you were under some specific and documented threats from Orlando Fletcher. Lastly, of course, your friend Ali here has shed some additional light."

*I had?* Did he mean that was a good thing? Or a bad thing?

I held my breath.

Judge Shapiro went on. "I am mandating six months of mental health counseling for you, twice a week," he said.

I saw Dee-Cee squeeze Zoe's hand, and I think I even saw Zoe's shoulders go down a few inches. This was good news.

"That order will be extendable to eighteen months at the discretion of your assigned counselor," he said. "I'm also going to require that you perform twenty hours of community service a month for the next twelve months. Do you understand?"

"Yes, your honor," Zoe said.

She was still getting punished, but at least she wasn't getting sent away to juvenile detention. I was glad for her, and *really* glad my testimony hadn't messed things up. Zoe and her mom were both crying, but happy tears this time, right in front of me.

Shapiro banged on the bench with his gavel. "That's it, ladies and gentlemen. This court is adjourned," he said.

And just like that, it was over.

# Chapter 45

Our big "My Washington" event at school came up pretty quick after that. Everyone in Mrs. Achebe's classes had put together something from their reports, either to present live onstage, or at tables in the hall.

For the live show, the auditorium was packed with parents, families, and other students. Mrs. Achebe had even set up a team of three kids as camera operators, so we could edit this whole thing into a video to put out in the community.

281

Patrice Shimm went first. I kind of expected her to give a boring speech, but she surprised us all by announcing that she was going to run for election to the City Council in Ward 6. No kid had ever done that in DC. I didn't know if she had any chance of winning, but I gave her a standing ovation along with everyone else, for sure.

Next, Eddie Cruz got up and said he was launching something called "The 2.5 Project." It was to raise awareness about how Black people are two and a half times more likely to be shot by police than other people. While he talked, he also showed a slideshow of stories about Black and Brown kids around the country who were doing the same kind of activism. I don't even *like* Eddie, but I've got to admit, it was pretty inspiring.

I had to give credit to Mrs. Achebe, too. She was the one always telling us how kids can accomplish anything they put their minds to. And so far, she was right. Hundred percent.

As for me, I think Mrs. A. was expecting some kind of talk about homelessness. Which is basically what I had planned, except I wasn't going to do most of the talking. Instead, I'd gotten Zoe's permission and invited her dad to come and let me interview him onstage. Mr. Knight was awesome, too, and answered all my questions about what it was like to live on the street, and how hard it could be, and also about how it can happen to anyone.

A little after that, it was Zoe's turn. She'd already told me and Ruby what she had planned, but I don't think anyone else knew about the bombshell she was about to drop.

"Hey y'all," she said. "First, I want to thank everyone at Wash Latin for the love and support when I was in the hospital, and with everything else that's been going on."

She got a big round of applause for that.

"I especially want to thank my little investigative team. I'm talking about Gabe, Cedric, Mateo, and of course, my girl, Ruby Sandoval. I love you guys," she said. "And...yeah, I'm saving the best for last."

I could feel my friends looking at me, and Ruby elbowed me in the side. My face got a little warmer, too.

"I just want to say," Zoe went on, "my boy Ali

over here stepped up for me in ways that some of you know about, and in other ways that you never will. But trust me when I say you should elect him class president. Or maybe give him the rest of the year off, cause he deserves it."

People laughed at that, and there was some more clapping. A couple people put their hands on my shoulders and jostled me around, too. I'm not going to say I felt like any kind of hero, but it *was* way better than a lot of what I'd been getting at school lately.

Still, I knew what else Zoe was getting ready to say, and I wasn't excited about it all.

"Anyway," she went on, "I hope nobody minds, but I actually have some news to share, and this is my last chance to do it, before...well, you'll see. Just listen up."

Adele Freeman and another one of Zoe's friends from choir came out then and stood behind her. They were both wearing pink scarves wrapped around their left arms, like Zoe's cast. Once they hit center stage, they started beatboxing, laying down a live track.

"This is called *My Washington*," Zoe said. Then she took the mike off the stand and jumped in.

Yo, yo, yo, listen up...listen up...
You know I've had it rough these days, it's been a heavy load,
But what I haven't told you is, I'm 'bout to hit the road.
We're packing up and moving out, to live some Cali style,
But don't you fret, I won't forget my sweet OG square mile.
DC is where my roots are at, I grew 'em down and deep.
I know this city inside out, I'd walk it in my sleep.
But even so, it's time to go, and time for me to say,
"Good-bye to you, my Washington, hello to you, LA."

285

Gabe, Cedric, and Mateo were giving me and Ruby wide eyes at that point. Nobody else knew until just then that Zoe was moving away. And while I was glad she'd let me in on the secret, like I said before, it wasn't what you'd call good news.

That's right, we're going Holly-
wood, I hear they've got nice
hills.
My momma, she'll be slaying it
while I work on my skills.
'Cause yeah, I messed up big-
time, and took too long to see,
The only one to blame in this
ain't nobody but me.
So now I own this mess for sure,
and yep, it's been too real.
But here's a fact: I'm bounc-
ing back! 'Cause like this arm,
I'll heal!

The backup girls had their scarves off now, sway-ing and waving them over their heads, like they'd turned those pretend casts into victory flags. Everyone else was on their feet, too, cheering Zoe along while she spit her last rhyme of the night.

That's it, that's what I came
to say, it's what Miss Z's
about,
And just like that, my Washington, I'm saying, "Zoe—OUT!"

# CHAPTER 46

BACK HOME AFTER the open house, we had a little party at our place for everyone. It was a celebration, for sure, but also a kind of good-bye party for Zoe and Dee-Cee, since they were leaving in a few days.

Dee-Cee brought a huge pecan pie. Nana made peach upside-down cake, and put out about six kinds of ice cream. Gabe's mom brought home-made chocolate truffles, too. It was like good, on top of great, on top of awesome.

The best part, though, was when Dee-Cee saw our piano on the back sunporch.

"Well, lookee here," she said. "Who plays this?"

"Dad does," I told her.

Dad was standing in the door of the porch, and Dee-Cee turned to look at him, then pointed back at the piano.

"Shall we?" she asked. And the look on Dad's face was like some rookie who had just gotten called up to the majors.

"How do you feel about Gershwin?" he said, sitting down at the keyboard.

Now it was Dee-Cee's turn to smile big. "You have good taste," she said. "Go ahead, Alex. I'll keep up."

Dad played one of Nana Mama's favorite songs, "Summertime," but in the style of Angélique Kidjo, who is one of his favorite singers. Dee-Cee tore it up, of course, and everyone yelled for more when they were done.

As they were starting up the next song, I looked around and realized there was one person missing. I didn't see Zoe anywhere.

So I went looking for her.

She wasn't in the dining room, or the living room. Then I checked upstairs. It seemed weird to think she might have gone into one of the bedrooms, but she hadn't. It wasn't until I was just about to head back down, when I heard Zoe's voice.

"Hey!"

"Hello?" I said.

"Out here."

I turned to look, and saw her outside the window at the end of the upstairs hall. While everyone was on the back porch listening to the music, Zoe had snuck out onto the front porch roof. Which was so her.

I went over and ducked out the window to sit next to her.

"What are you doing up here?" I asked.

"Just thinking," she said.

"About what?"

"About how I'm going to miss you when we go," she said. "It doesn't really seem fair."

I didn't think so, either. Just when Zoe and I were getting this stuff behind us, and before I could even figure out if she was my girlfriend, they were moving away. I could understand why, but man, I hated it.

"I'll miss you, too," I said, and put her hand in mine.

It was nice out there, looking down at the street and up at the sky. We could hear Dad playing, and Dee-Cee singing "Eleanor Rigby" downstairs, while the party kept going without us.

"The judge said I can do that counseling and community service out in LA. Momma just has to sign some paperwork, and notify the court about where it will be happening. Then we're good to go," Zoe said.

"What about Kim?" I asked.

"She and Momma aren't speaking right now, but they'll work it out," Zoe said. "Orlando got three months. She broke it off with him even before that, though. Now that he's out of the picture, it might turn out okay."

"Do you think I'll ever see you again?" I asked.

"Sure," Zoe said. "Momma's touring all the time. And besides, I hear they have these things called airplanes. Supposedly, people fly them to LA every day."

"Don't make me laugh right now," I said. "I'm kind of busy being sad about this."

"Just sayin'. You should come visit," she told me. "Like...please do."

I looked over at her, and she looked back, and we kissed. One more time.

"I've always wanted to go to California," I said.

Zoe leaned her head against my shoulder. "Then I guess I'll see you there," she told me.

I smiled in the dark, and just let the silence ride a little bit. I was really sorry she was leaving, but at the same time, I was glad to be sitting up on that roof with her. For now, anyway, I was exactly where I wanted to be.

It's like Nana says. If you look closely enough, no matter what else is going on, and how complicated things might get, you can always find something to be grateful for. And you can always find a reason to say...

Life is good.

Discover the next exciting instalment
in the Ali Cross series . . .

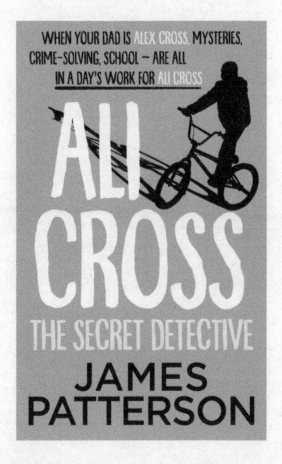

Turn the page for a sneak preview . . .

# CHAPTER 1

I'M GOING TO start by telling you about my friend Gabe Qualls. He's a part-time middle school student, and a full-time genius. Because he's a genius, he's always inventing things. And because we're such good friends, he's always sharing the inventions with me.

Just last week he perfected one of his best inventions ever. It arrived at the best possible time. You see, I haven't had a decent real adventure in what feels like a hundred years. I've been hurting for something exciting to happen. And Gabe's new invention is practically a guarantee that something big will happen.

Here's what it is. A cell phone that lets me intercept police calls.

Wait. Wait. Wait. It's nothing bad. Nothing illegal. I mean, come on. My father is Detective Alex Cross. With him as a dad, I've got to be extra careful.

Here's the deal. Gabe figured out how to make an app that actually transcribes and summarizes local police radio chatter in real time. (Don't ask me how he did it. *He's* the total computer genius. Not me.)

But here's the coolest part. Gabe secretly hooked it up to the Washington, DC, Metropolitan Police scanner. And he set it so if the cops say certain key words, or if they're headed somewhere in our neighborhood, it sends a ridiculously loud text alert to both our phones. So whenever there's an emergency call in Southeast—the part of the city where me and my family live—we're the first two to hear about it.

Which means we can get to the crime scene, fast.

Oh, it works well—really well. In fact, I'm in a

2

deep cozy sleep this morning and...there it is now. Loud. Blaring.

I look at my phone. 3:35 a.m. The screen simply says:

**Stanton Houses. Emergency situ. Group.**

Group? What does that mean? Gabe really needs to work on an in-app translator for the police lingo.

Moaning just a little, I stumble out of bed and slip into my jeans and a ratty gray T-shirt. I've chased after three police calls so far this past week. A stolen car, an attempted robbery, and a boring noise complaint. Each one had potential, but they all turned out to be duds.

I'm hoping this new call is an exciting one.

Chasing police calls is kind of a weird hobby, right? Most of my friends play video games. Or sports. Or make goofball TikTok videos.

Me? I like to check out crime scenes. Let me rephrase that. Checking out crime scenes, looking into police cases, well, that's about the coolest thing I can imagine.

Why do I do it? I guess you could say it's in my DNA. Yeah. That's it. But even if that's the reason,

I don't think the guy responsible for that DNA, my dad, would be cool with me following in his footsteps, especially since I'm still in middle school. Crime, guns, bad guys. It can be a dangerous job.

Which is why I'm forced to sneak out of the house. *Shhhh.*

Holding my dirty Puma Clydes in my hand, I soft-step down the stairs and tiptoe out the door. If I wake him or my stepmom Bree, I'm dead. My family, you see, is pretty good at hearing stuff, seeing stuff, and, like me, gently nosing into one another's stuff.

Luckily, this time, they all seem to be sleeping like a bunch of babies.

I wait till I'm a whole block from my own house before I call Gabe.

"Are you ready to go?" I ask.

I can tell from his grumpy voice that Gabe hasn't moved since *his* own police scanner alert went off.

"It's like three o'clock in the morning, Ali," he says.

I fight his grumpy with the best friend card.

"C'mon, man. You wouldn't let me go alone,

4

would you?" There's an address on the screen now. I read the message to him, "Group disturbance at 1916 18th SE."

Then I tease him a little. I can't help it.

"Come on, Gabe. It's your favorite part of town."

"Public housing? The Stanton Houses? My favorite part?"

"Yeah," I answer. "It's right across the street from the *library*."

"Funny stuff, Ali. Nothing like a nerd-genius joke at three in the morning."

"Just get your butt over there," I say. "Now."

"It's probably just like the others. A big nothing deal," Gabe says.

I know Gabe could be right. Maybe this call *will* turn out to be another dud.

But for some reason, I have a feeling it's going to be a big one.

# CHAPTER 2

GABE AND I meet up. The genius looks like he's still dressed for bed—red boxers sticking out from over green gym shorts, along with a red and white striped T-shirt.

"What's up, Christmas tree?" I say.

"Huh?" He doesn't get the joke. Or at least he pretends not to.

We hustle over toward the crime scene. It's not hard to find. It's all flashing lights and megaphones. It's a nasty mix of police shouts and wailing sirens.

Then we plant ourselves at the side of the library for the perfect view.

"This looks pretty serious," I say.

"Uh, you think so?" Gabe says. "What gave it away? The eight police cars or the forty people crowding around?"

I guess I am a master of the obvious.

"It's got to be something with the gangs," Gabe says.

As soon as Gabe mentions the word *gangs*, I tell him what my dad once said.

"If you can bust the gangs, you can build the city."

"Man, it would take a lot of busting and a lot of building," Gabe says, and as I look across the street at the twisted window bars and graffiti on the Stanton Houses, I know what he means.

The biggest problems with the gangs are the feuds between the gangs themselves. The fights can be brutal—guns, fists, knives, even rocks are used. They're started over turf disputes or drugs or someone's girlfriend or boyfriend.

Police are leading a few folks out of the building.

It's pretty clear that these are residents of the houses. Adults wearing nightgowns and underwear and sweatpants. Little kids in pajamas.

The police rush this small group to a spot behind one of the barricades. Then we hear a guy on a megaphone talking to the people watching from the surrounding houses: "PLEASE REMAIN IN YOUR HOMES. PLEASE REMAIN IN YOUR HOMES. POLICE WILL INFORM YOU WHEN IT'S SAFE TO LEAVE."

"That'll sure scare you," Gabe says.

I check my phone screen. "No updates on the event," I tell Gabe. "I think we should remain in our current position."

Gabe rolls his eyes. His voice is really sarcastic as he says, "Yes, sir. Whatever you say, Sergeant Ali." Before I can tell Gabe to go, we see a sudden parade of people coming out the side door of the apartment.

Three of those people—two guys, one woman—are clicked into handcuffs. It looks like stuff you see in news clips. The police stare straight ahead while they walk. The suspects are pushing their chins into their chests as far as they can. I watch closely as the handcuffed people are escorted by an even mix of four uniformed cops and four plainclothes.

Okay. I'm excited, excited enough that I decide to move in closer to the front of the crowd.

"Cool it, man," Gabe says as he tugs at the back of my shirt. "The police don't want any interference from two punk teenagers."

Gabe is right. Plus, a few of the officers and detectives might actually recognize me. I've been down at headquarters a few times with my dad. We move back a little, a pretty bad attempt at camouflage.

Three police cars pull up to the side of the building where the action is.

"Three perps. Three arrests. Three squad cars," I say. "Everybody gets their own chauffeur. This must be serious."

"Hey, Ali. Look at the second guy," Gabe says. He sounds anxious.

"Lower your voice, man," I say. He doesn't really talk any quieter. Instead he talks in the kind of whisper you could hear a few yards away.

"On the right. On the right," he says. "Look at the second guy on the right."

I squint. I look.

Oh, damn! Damn and damn it again.

"Let's move," I say. We bend over, put our heads down, and we look exactly like what we are—two scared, stupid kids trying to hide.

"You said they were all asleep when you left your house," Gabe says.

"They were. At least I thought they were," I answer.

"Man, you better hope he doesn't look this way. Nobody can fool your father."

"Least of all, me," I say.

# CHAPTER 3

THE POLICE LOAD the three people into three separate patrol cars that flip on their sirens and drive off. It's kind of interesting to watch how the officers handle the three people that they're bringing in. They're not really rough with them. There's no shoving or pushing. But they're firm also. I'd call them confident but polite. I do notice that one of the officers does not do the usual "watch-your-head" move when they put their guy into the car.

I wonder, is that a television thing? Or is it an actual rule, that the officer just broke?

I'm pretty sure that Gabe and I are far enough away that nobody can see us. And my father wasn't really looking around; he seemed very preoccupied with walking with, watching, and guiding his suspect.

I don't even realize I've been holding my breath until he gets into an unmarked car and drives off, too.

"We can move in closer now," I say.

"Yeah," says Gabe. "Now that the big guy is gone."

I'm not sure, but I'm not liking Gabe calling my father "the big guy." It's not exactly disrespectful. And, okay, the name sort of fits. But my friend's voice has a little scorn to it. Maybe. Yeah, maybe. It could be I'm just too sensitive.

Anyway, as we cross the street, I scope out the crowd. I'm guessing most of these people are from the Stanton Houses. Probably some are what the police call "lookie-loos," the people who gather around when there's a car accident, a fire, or even an extra-dangerous crime scene, like a shooting. Why watch Netflix when you can watch real life?

A really old guy standing next to Gabe, smoking a pipe, says, "You kids from the neighborhood?"

"Yeah, pretty close by," I say.

"But not *that* close," Gabe says. I don't know what he's worried about that he has to add that little bit. Not that the old guy seems to care.

"Bad stuff is always going on around here," says the old guy. "Nobody can stop it."

"It's the gangs again," says a woman who's holding a very unhappy baby. The baby is screaming loud enough that she could actually drown out the sirens on the police cars that are speeding away.

The woman talks over her baby. "He's right. It's the same as always. The gangs fight. Some of 'em get arrested. But nothing changes. Same old story." Then she adds, "I wish all the gangs would just kill each other already. Then we'd be done with it."

The old guy nods his head.

"Sometimes it seems that that's exactly what they're trying to do. Kill each other," says the old guy. "Can't say as I'd be heartbroken if they all ended up dead."

I want to cry out, "What are you, crazy? What kind of solution is that?"

"Cops'd just as soon let them run around as shoot them," says the young mother.

"Cops don't care," says the old man.

Okay, my blood is at boiling level now. I want to say, "The police try really hard to keep things under control. And—you know what—the cops I know *do* care."

But then I realize...damn it. I understand the old guy. I understand the woman with the baby. And what I understand is that this whole situation sucks.

"Well, you got your wish tonight," says another woman in the crowd. She's wearing purple eyeglasses and has her hair in curlers.

"Yeah," she says. "The police shot one of the gang members. Blood. Guts. The whole thing. The ambulance just left ten minutes ago, and look," she says. "It's already on the news."

Hang on. A police shooting? The woman holds

up her cell phone. A television title says, POLICE SHOOTING IN SOUTHEAST. GANG WARS!

Everything inside me shifts. My stomach knots up. My brain has trouble focusing.

"Who was it?" I say. "Did they say if it was a cop in uniform?"

"You know as much as I know," says the woman.

The browser switches to a different piece of news, some new headline about corruption in the Baltimore judicial system. Damn. Is there ever anything good in the news?

Gabe asks, "You sure they didn't mention who..."

The lady with the phone doesn't even let him finish the sentence. She says, "Are you boys listening? Like I said, you know as much as I do."

My stomach knot is only getting tighter.

I tell Gabe that we should be leaving.

He nods.

I can see that he has the same worry I do: that the cop who fired the gun might have been my dad.

## ALSO BY JAMES PATTERSON

### MIDDLE SCHOOL SERIES

### I FUNNY SERIES

## MAX EINSTEIN SERIES

The Genius Experiment (*with Chris Grabenstein*)
Rebels with a Cause (*with Chris Grabenstein*)
Saves the Future (*with Chris Grabenstein*)
World Champions! (*with Chris Grabenstein*)

## DOG DIARIES SERIES

Dog Diaries (*with Steven Butler*)
Happy Howlidays! (*with Steven Butler*)
Mission Impawsible (*with Steven Butler*)
Curse of the Mystery Mutt (*with Steven Butler*)
Camping Chaos! (*with Steven Butler*)
Dinosaur Disaster! (*with Steven Butler*)
Big Top Bonanza! (*with Steven Butler*)

## HOUSE OF ROBOTS SERIES

House of Robots (*with Chris Grabenstein*)
Robots Go Wild! (*with Chris Grabenstein*)
Robot Revolution (*with Chris Grabenstein*)

## JACKY HA-HA SERIES

Jacky Ha-Ha (*with Chris Grabenstein*)
My Life is a Joke (*with Chris Grabenstein*)

## OTHER ILLUSTRATED NOVELS

Kenny Wright: Superhero (*with Chris Tebbetts*)
Homeroom Diaries (*with Lisa Papademetriou*)

Word of Mouse (*with Chris Grabenstein*)

Pottymouth and Stoopid (*with Chris Grabenstein*)

Laugh Out Loud (*with Chris Grabenstein*)

Not So Normal Norbert (*with Joey Green*)

Unbelievably Boring Bart (*with Duane Swierczynski*)

Katt vs. Dogg (*with Chris Grabenstein*)

Scaredy Cat (*with Chris Grabenstein*)

Best Nerds Forever (*with Chris Grabenstein*)

Katt Loves Dogg (*with Chris Grabenstein*)

## DANIEL X SERIES

The Dangerous Days of Daniel X (*with Michael Ledwidge*)

Watch the Skies (*with Ned Rust*)

Demons and Druids (*with Adam Sadler*)

Game Over (*with Ned Rust*)

Armageddon (*with Chris Grabenstein*)

Lights Out (*with Chris Grabenstein*)

For more information about James Patterson's novels,
visit www.penguin.co.uk

# THE FIRST BOOK IN THE ALI CROSS SERIES

## ALI CROSS
## JAMES PATTERSON

Ali Cross knows Gabe Qualls better than anyone, so when his friend goes missing, Ali jumps right into action. Alex Cross has taught his son the values he needs to solve the mystery: intelligence, persistence, and logic. One thing Ali hasn't learned? Patience.

Because Ali realises that with every day that passes without the police finding Gabe, the less likely it is that he'll ever be found. And being Alex Cross's son, he refuses to accept those odds.

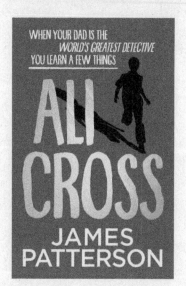